The Wolf of Wilmore Manor

Kieran Wiesenberg

For rights inquiries, permissions, or additional information, please contact:

info@kieranwiesenberg.com

www.kieranwiesenberg.com

The Wolf of Wilmore Manor / Kieran Wiesenberg. — First edition

ISBN 979-8-9860007-3-2

Cover illustration and design by Kieran Wiesenberg

For Mom and Dad

Chapter One

The Invitation

"I know you're not a real wolf," the kid said, looking up at Julian, face all smeared with pizza sauce and cake frosting. "You're just some guy in a costume."

Julian struggled to find the child through the eyeholes of his character suit. They got kids like this every once in a while. Pre-tweens who ripped the charade apart despite being the ones who'd asked for it. Mostly it was futile to try and argue with them, but Julian went for it anyway. He put on his best Willy voice.

"Guy in a costume?" he said, throwing his arms up in an exaggerated gesture. "The only guy in a costume I see is you!" As he said this, he gave a tug to the boy's birthday hat, making it jump on his head. "I'm Willy Wolfgang, and I'm here to celebrate your ninth birthday!"

Julian did a little dance then, the result of which made the head of his costume turn a bit on his shoulders, disorienting him. By the time he got it back into place, the kid was gone.

"It's my tenth birthday!" came a shrill voice from behind him. "And if you were the real Willy Wolfgang, you'd *know*!"

Sharp pain suddenly as the ten-year-old's sneaker connected with Julian's crotch. For all the padding within the Willy Wolfgang suit, there seemed to have been none dedicated to the area between the legs. Julian's pain was matched in its intensity only by his disbelief.

He kicked me. The little bastard kicked me.

The anger swell and child hunt that would have ensued were both abated only by Sarah's voice.

"Okay!" she said. "That's enough time with Willy today. Why doesn't everyone head back out to the arcade for some more game time!"

There was a rumbling of footsteps and the slamming of a door and suddenly the room was quiet, freed from the ambience of a fifth grade class' worth of pre-tweens. Julian tore his Willy head off without making sure the coast was clear. At the moment, he didn't exactly care about ruining childhoods.

He wiped his sweaty, ruffled hair out of his face to find an abandoned room full of pizza-stained paper plates and Sarah standing at the door looking back at him. She was giving him that look she always did when there was a particularly rowdy party, and Julian just shook his head. He crossed to the opposite side of the room and slid down the wall until he was on the floor, Willy head sitting large and decapitated in his lap.

"That kid kicked me in the balls, Sarah," he said after a moment.

"I saw," she said. "Do you want to talk about it?"

Julian just shook his head. "Not really. How long until six?"

"It's eleven."

Julian could only sigh.

He was about to say something more when a knock came from the door leading out to the arcade. Instinctively moving to redon the Willy head, Julian stopped when Sarah opened the door and the knocker was revealed to be not a child, but a man.

A mailman.

He was an older, healthy-looking gentleman dressed in the regular garb, and he gave each of the two employees a friendly smile.

"Letter for Julian Schultz?" he said, holding up a white envelope.

"That's me," Julian said, rising from the ground. The mailman met him halfway, placed the letter in Julian's gloved hand without comment and turned away.

"Have a nice day!" he said.

"You too," Sarah said, shutting the door behind him. She turned back to Julian with a confused look. "Since when do you get your mail delivered here at work?"

Julian shrugged. "Past few weeks or so."

Sarah's brow narrowed further. "Why not just have it sent to your apartment?"

Julian's eyes fell to the ground. "Oh, yeah, so...I'm actually not living there anymore," he said, scratching nervously at the back of his head. "Rent went up and well...money being so tight and all..."

"Oh," Sarah said, features loosening. "I'm sorry. Are you...looking for another place?"

"Ah, not at the moment, no. Figured it'd be easier to just live out of the car for a while. Give me some time to save up a little and get back on my feet."

Sarah nodded solemnly. It looked like she wanted to ask more, though she must have sensed Julian's embarrassment and dropped it.

"Who's the letter from?" she asked instead, voice rising at the change of subject.

"No one I know," Julian said, narrowing his eyes at the envelope.

"Well, what's the name?"

***

"Valentina Wilmore?" Suzie said, raising an eyebrow as she tossed the letter onto the counter. "Who's Valentina Wilmore?"

From his kitchen counter turned workbench, Nicholas Chau took a moment to squint at the pale envelope before returning his attention to the disassembled camera in front of him.

"No idea," he said.

"Well, she obviously knows who *you* are," Suzie teased, tapping the red-penned words along the letter's front. It was addressed to Nicholas directly. A smirk curved up one side of her lips. "Sure it's not your mistress?"

Nicholas laughed. "Definitely not."

"I don't know," Suzie said, eyeing the letter with mock suspicion. "I think it is. I think the famous Nicholas Chau has just been caught red-handed in a *scandalous* love affair!"

"Scandalous, eh?" Nicholas said, still smiling.

"Mm-hm."

There was a high-pitched whine as a previously dim light on the camera suddenly whirred back to life. Satisfied, Nicholas returned his attention to the letter.

"Can I read it?" Suzie asked, practically beaming.

"Of course," Nicholas said, handing her the multi-tool he'd been using on the camera. "That is, if you think you can handle the heart-wrenching truth of my infidelity."

"I'll do my best," she said with a smile, though as she began to read the letter, her expression quickly turned to that of confusion.

"What?" Nicholas asked. "What does it say?"

***

Dear Mr. Proctor,

I am contacting you regarding an opportunity in which you might take both personal and professional interest.

I believe that I have captured a werewolf in the flesh.

As proof, I have included within this envelope a lock of its pelt. I trust that it, in addition to my contacting of you, specifically, will verify both the validity of my claim and the soundness of my intentions.

Along with yourself, I have contacted a several other persons whom I believe may take a similar interest in this matter, and hereby extend this invitation to you all. My family lays claim to an estate in the Adirondack region of New York state. It is here where I found the specimen, and it is here where I hope to present it to you all.

I wish only for a weekend of private merriment and study ahead of my unveiling this discovery to the wider world. I do hope you will take the opportunity, as well as this invitation, in the good faith with which both were given. Specific times and locations, including my address and transportation instructions, are included on the page opposite.

I hope to see you soon.

Signed,
Ms. Valentina Wilmore

After finishing the letter, Esteban Proctor turned his eyes to the envelope on the nightstand, and to the lock of gray hair that had fallen out of it. Raising the clump to his nose, he felt a familiar musk run up his nostrils.

It was wolf all right.

He read the letter again and then a third time, turning it over to read the location details on the back.

"Hm," he said finally. And that was all he said.

Shoving the letter and the lock back into the envelope and that into a jacket pocket, he picked his hat up off the motel bedspread and made for the door.

***

"It's just for the weekend, Coach. Come practice Monday, I'll be back and ready to go."

Yusuf Miller sat uncomfortably in the humid train car, go-bag in his lap, cell phone pressed tight to his ear. He'd always hated the ride into the city, felt like the chairs were always a bit too small for his large frame. Couple that with the August heat and an aching body from working out all week, and the only thing that could have been worse was Coach Kittredge screaming in his ear...which he was.

"Come practice Monday, you better be ready to go and *glow*," came his tinny voice over the cell phone speaker. "With the games we've got coming up, there's going to be no room for error. Just how I let you convince me that some late-August trip upstate was a good idea I *still* don't know."

"Don't worry, Coach," Yusuf said. "If this trip goes how I think it will, it'll be a win for the whole school. Something to put Willsbury on the map. This is *bigger* than football."

It was true. Yusuf loved the game, of course. Loved playing for the Willsbury Wolves and even for Coach Kittredge. Football had secured him his scholarship and had so far been the ticket to everything great in his life. And it was a great life, though admittedly...he'd always felt like there was something missing. Like there was something more out there for him. Some untapped potential he'd had yet to identify. Whatever that potential was, it had long eluded him, though if this weekend really did go how Yusuf was hoping it would, he had a feeling he might just be able to catch a glimpse.

"There you go with that 'bigger than football' line," said Kittredge. "In case you haven't noticed, Miller, in my world, there ain't *nothing* bigger. Not even close!"

"And that's why you're going to win coach of the year this year."

Kittredge laughed. "Not if my star quarterback gets injured on some mysterious bender a week before the season opener!"

"Like I said, Coach, it's an *academic* trip. Don't worry. I'll be fine."

"You better be. Keep in touch, will you?"

"Of course."

"All right, well...have a good time then."

"You too, Coach. Try to relax, yeah?"

Kittredge laughed again. "You're funny," he said, and ended the call.

Yusuf was left to his thoughts, silently watching the other passengers as the train zipped its way toward the airport. His eyes landed on a girl near his age with dark hair and darker clothes. She was pretty, though not the type he usually dated. She sat at the very end of the car, large headphones over her ears, quietly doodling something in a sketchbook. Absently, he wondered what it was.

***

Rowan Dobrzynski was putting the finishing touches on a sketch when she noticed the big guy staring at her. She looked up and he quickly turned away, buried his nose in his phone before peeking up again. When he did, she smiled at him, and he smiled back.

He was cute, though not the type she usually dated. Too muscular. Too jock. She returned her attention to her sketchbook and found a black-and-white werewolf staring back at her.

She usually never drew them, werewolves. She wasn't sure why. Maybe because they were too easy. Uninteresting or uninspired. She usually never drew them, though lately, she'd been drawing nothing else. Ever since that mysterious letter had arrived in her mailbox, since the mysterious Valentina Wilmore had extended her invitation, promising a werewolf in three dimensions and full color.

A proud homebody, Rowan usually never traveled either, though that too was in flux—the reason being that she'd made a promise. She'd promised herself that she'd take an opportunity like this should one ever present itself, and here was this one having practically fallen right into her lap.

She still wasn't sure how this Valentina Wilmore had found her. Her online following was certainly growing, though even Rowan could admit that it was still minuscule compared to many of her favorite artists. That she'd been chosen out of anyone...it seemed so random. Or rather...it seemed like *fate*.

It was a good thing, she reassured herself as she started onto a new page. An opportunity to get out of her comfort zone and challenge herself. She would be taking a plane, for one, and she'd never done that before.

***

It was Damian Donegan's five-hundredth plane ride. With the particular airline, that is. He knew because the app had congratulated him for it and given him a coupon for a first class ticket. A whole 5% discount.

How generous, he'd thought.

Of course, he hadn't taken it, though as he tottered up the ramp, ass already sore from having sat in the airport for an hour, he began to wish he had.

He traveled a lot for work, giving various lectures and book talks at schools and universities around the country. Usually, that meant the schools paying for his airfare, and—in the case of the more prestigious ones—that usually also meant first class. Such were the perks of academia, though on this particular venture, they did not totally apply.

This was not a work trip—was not even a trip to a school or university. No, this was a trip to a mysterious estate halfway across the country on the invitation of a cryptic and as-of-yet unknown benefactor. The idea that anyone of Damian's professional standing would have submitted to such a request, and at the start of the semester, no less, was outrageous.

Though Damian had not hesitated.

There'd been something about that letter. Something about the mysterious Valentina Wilmore and her fantastical promise that had intrigued him, that had sunk its werewolf fangs deep into his psyche and refused to let go. And so he'd gone limp to its kill shake. He'd packed his suitcase, put on his best tweed coat, and bought his own ticket at full price.

That is, *economy* full price.

It was a professional trip, of course. Something that would prove beneficial to his research if not form the basis of his next book. So far as his chair and the rest of the board were concerned, that was all it was. Though it was a personal trip too. And only Damian knew to what extent.

A werewolf in the flesh? An assortment of guests with similar interests? He could only wonder at the possibilities. That he'd been able to pitch it as a research trip had been but a lucky coincidence. Truthfully, Damian would have said just about anything to get them to let him go. Might have *done* just about anything too.

Including flying economy.

As he shuffled past the first class passengers, he tried not to let his envy overtake him. He tried to make his excitement for the trip overpower his dread for sitting in a cramped middle seat for four long hours, though it was slow to go. He caught sight of a pretty, dark-skinned woman in the last first class seat, a large laptop fitted comfortably within her spacious surroundings, and he couldn't stop the scowl that curved over his face.

Oh, how he wished that were him.

***

Nora Inwood paid no attention to the gray-haired man shooting her a sour look as he scooted past into the business section. Her nose was buried far too deep in her laptop for that, her attention far too fixated on the anatomy of wolves.

On the anatomy of *werewolves*.

The theoretical anatomy of werewolves, that is. Them being the stuff of legend—make-believe fantasy and all—there was an unsurprising lack of true zoological data to be found. Timber and dire wolves, sure. You could fill an entire library with the stuff. But *were*wolves? *Lycanthropes?* Genuine moon-shifting *loups-garous*? Such studies had been forever confined to the fiction section.

Nora wondered if this upcoming weekend might change that.

For Nora, the letter could not have come at a better time. For the past six months, since Dr. Vaillancourt had relocated to Wisconsin, it had been just her and the nurses at the clinic...and about a million sick or injured animals in between. Of course, she loved taking care of them, had become a vet for the very reason, but the 60-hour work weeks had been adding up, and she was ready for a break. Ready for a *vacation*. And though her first pick likely would have been somewhere slightly more exotic than upstate New York, something about the letter she'd received made her think that this particular trip might just be worth the lack of beach.

Might just be worth *everything*.

As she continued to peruse her various anatomical diagrams, a man's voice suddenly sounded over the plane's intercom.

"Good morning, ladies and gentlemen, this is your captain speaking. We're going to be taking off very shortly here. Just wanted to jump on here and say that we're currently experiencing a slight delay due to an adjacent flight taking off on our runway. Looks like that's flight number...um...hold on...oh, that's not a plane. Sorry folks, it seems we've been cut off by a...private jet?"

***

Amelia Hyde sat alone in the large, well-furnished cabin of her private jet, more or less unaware of the fact that they were taking off. She'd been flying so much lately, jetting back-and-forth between different premieres and filming locations that the wonder of it rarely struck her anymore. The view of the city from above was always enrapturing, of course, though this morning she paid it no notice. The latest Elijah Vaughn novel sat in her lap, and it was within its pages where her focus remained.

Mostly.

Despite her eyes staying on the pages, her thoughts had been consistently straying elsewhere. Beyond the werewolves of fiction and to the ones of her near future. Or so she hoped.

Could it be true? She found herself wondering. *Could this mysterious Valentina Wilmore have actually captured a werewolf?*

What could it mean? Who could that person—or that wolf—be? Who were the other guests invited? And what did it all mean for Amelia?

She didn't know yet, though her gut tickled with a nervous anticipation.

After another moment, she closed the book with a sigh, leaving it to rest on the cabin's side table. As much as she wanted to read it, she knew she wouldn't be able to give it her full attention right now. And a new Elijah Vaughn novel was definitely something that warranted one's full attention. Especially when that one was an actress on contract to reprise her role for the upcoming adaptation.

Amelia would read it later, when her head wasn't so filled with questions, and when the mystery of this weekend in upstate New York had been solved.

She was grateful that the flight was only a few hours. Had she been forced to sit with the anticipation for any longer, she thought she might explode. Absently, she began to wonder about the other guests, and if any of their commutes had been longer.

***

Elijah Vaughn had been on the road for four days. It was a 36-hour drive from downstate Arizona to upstate New York, and the author had loved every minute of it.

Upon receiving his letter from the mysterious Valentina Wilmore, he'd known instantly that he'd be accepting her invitation. That he'd gotten it in time to make a cross-country road trip of the affair had only been a plus.

Elijah was in the planning stage of his next book, his fourteenth altogether, and so he'd been hoping to get on the road anyway. Driving was always where he got his best ideas. In fact, he couldn't recall a single book he'd written whose plot hadn't come together overtop the spinning of his wheels on the interstate. With an endless gray horizon in front of him, and a million of those little white lines whipping behind, it seemed like there was nothing his mind couldn't conquer.

He'd made some progress on the new book this trip, had fleshed out some key plot points and character beats he hadn't had before, though if he was being honest, the drive had not been as productive as usual. Too many thoughts of the destination in store. Not bad thoughts per say, but not wholly good ones either.

A werewolf in the flesh?

Elijah wrote about werewolves for a living, knew more about them than the average Joe, and felt absolutely no shame in his identity as an enthusiast. But, even still...seeing one up close? A *real* one? And with others of similar interests? He still wasn't exactly sure what that meant, and even less if it was a good idea.

It was strange because, at least at first, he'd been entirely on board—had felt nothing but excitement for the unorthodox prospects. But then, the further he'd driven, the more he'd watched the desert die and the forest slowly rise in its place, the worse he'd begun to feel about the whole thing.

He was real close now, shoulder-deep in Adirondack country. With all the trees and mountains around him, the setting could have been ripped straight out of one of his novels. And while the imaginative part of his brain was loving it, the survivalist part had its hackles up. As familiar as the forest might have been to his characters, it was all but alien to Elijah. An unknown landscape he'd only ever fictionalized. That his fiction tended to be of the horror kind—the forests within always dark and dangerous and filled with monsters—didn't help much.

He managed to keep the worst thoughts away with some soft rock tunes on the radio, though as the sun dipped lower and lower behind the mountains, the deepening shadows were hard to ignore.

Eventually he came to the meeting spot, though. And for the first time in nearly five days, Elijah was not alone.

There were four people in the designated pull-off, three men and a woman. A collection of vehicles sat against the treeline behind them. Elijah parked his car beside these and was soon making introductions.

The tallest of the men approached him first, an older gentleman of the academic sort.

"Hello there," he said, calling out with a voice as large as his frame. "Are you another guest of Ms. Wilmore?"

"Just here for the werewolf convention," Elijah joked, shouldering his backpack.

"Right," the man said, not smiling. It seemed he was all business. "Come along then, meet the rest."

He hurriedly led Elijah to the center of the pull-off, to where the rest were gathered.

"Now then," he said, turning on a heel to face him. "If you wouldn't mind introducing yourself so that we might know how best to address you?"

"Sure," Elijah said, giving a nod to the strangers before him. "Name's Elijah. Elijah Vaughn."

"Good to meet you, Mr. Vaughn," the older man said, giving Elijah's hand a vigorous shake. "I am Dr. Damian Donegan, professor of anthropology at Breccan Augustus."

"Pleasure," Elijah said.

"All mine, Mr. Vaughn, all mine. Now then, from left to right, allow me to first introduce Mr. Nicholas Chau."

"Hey, how's it going?" said a friendly-looking man to Elijah's left. He wore dark-brimmed glasses and had a large camera hanging from a strap around his neck.

"And then there's Mr. Esteban Proctor," the professor continued, gesturing to the second man in the lineup.

This man was taller than Chau, with longer hair and rugged, handsome features. He wore a brown cowboy hat and regarded Elijah with dark, suspicious eyes. Upon Damian's introduction, he gave but a small nod and looked on.

"And lastly, Ms. Nora Inwood," Damian said, referring to the sole female of the group. She was a pretty woman about Elijah's age, with dark skin and long, braided hair.

"Elijah Vaughn?" she said, beaming with excitement. "As in, *A Howling Over Bloomington*, Elijah Vaughn?"

"That's me," Elijah said with a smile.

"Ahh!" she exclaimed, scrunching her hands in excitement. "I'm such a big fan! Gosh, I must have read each of your books at least ten times!"

Elijah laughed. "I'm so glad you enjoyed them."

"A writer, are you?" Damian said, seeming to size him up again. "Tell me, have you any academic pieces?"

Elijah shook his head. "Just fiction."

"Werewolf fiction, was it?"

"The *werewolfiest*."

"Right...well, should you ever require real-world inspiration for your fantastical stories, I might recommend my *own* work."

"You write about werewolves too?" Nora asked.

"And every other creature of mythology and folklore. It is my anthropological area of expertise. The study of humans through stories and legend."

"Cool," Elijah said genuinely. "So is that why we're all here? Each of us with our own connection to werewolves?"

"Well, I don't know about me," Nora said with a frown. "I mean, I love werewolves in books and movies, but then...that's not really a unique connection, is it?"

"Not alone, maybe," Damian said. "Though I fear you sell yourself entirely too short. Remind us again, if you will, of your profession?"

"Oh, well, I'm a veterinarian."

"Precisely," he continued. "Now tell us this: have you ever practiced veterinary medicine or provided care to a wolf?"

"Actually...yes," Nora said after a moment. She seemed to shift nervously. "It was just once, though."

"Just once would do it," Damian concluded with a nod. "And, assuming the extent of your work with canines, I might go as far as to say that your connection to both the ascendent wolf and mythological werewolf is—at least by proxy—the greatest of us all!" He turned his eyes to the other two men. "That is, unless Mr. Chau or Proctor have connections which supersede even that?"

"I do wildlife photography," Nicholas said, raising his camera with a hand, and he nodded before the question could be asked. "I've snapped some pictures of wolves before. I guess that fits."

"Most perfectly," Damian said with a nod, and his eyes then shifted expectantly to Proctor. All eyes did, though even after a moment of silence, the rugged man said nothing.

"Mr. Proctor?" Damian urged.

The man's eyes moved to the professor's without a word.

"Would you mind sharing with us what it is that you do?"

"Hunter," came his gruff reply, and the word was preceded by a wad of spit hitting the ground.

"A hunter!" Damian exclaimed. "Yes, I'd say that certainly fits too. And, if you wouldn't mind, what exactly is it you hunt?"

Proctor's eyes met everyone's before replying, a single word spoken through the ghost of a grin.

"Monsters."

Before anyone could reply, a sound from the woods diverted the group's attention. There was a rustling coming from the adjacent treeline, hushed voices and crunching footsteps, the sounds of someone approaching. Of someones.

The noises peaked as two figures emerged from the woods, together a mismatched duo, though no more so than the group already gathered. A man and woman, both looked college-age, though it was here where their similarities ended. The man was tall and muscular, with light brown skin and an erect, confident posture. The woman was small and thin, with a pale complexion that contrasted sharply with her all-black wardrobe. Upon emerging, the man immediately made for the group, closing the distance with long, powerful strides as the woman followed more slowly, a black bag clutched tightly at her side.

"Oh, yes, and here is the rest of our party," Damian said, beckoning to the two as they arrived.

"How you doing?" said the muscular young man, immediately extending an open hand to Elijah.

"Good, you?" Elijah said, shaking it. His grip was so far the firmest of all.

"Great. Name's Yusuf." He turned to the girl behind. "This is Rowan."

"Hi," she said, offering a kind but timid smile.

"Nice to meet you," Elijah said, nodding to them both. His eyes trailed down to the front of Yusuf's shirt, a blue jersey with a gray beast across the front.

"Willsbury Wolves?"

"About an hour north of Poughkeepsie," he said with a nod. "D1 football."

"You play?"

"Starting quarterback," he said with a grin.

"Another wolf," Nicholas said, putting words to Elijah's own thoughts. At Yusuf's look of confusion, Damian explained.

"We were just admiring a common thread between us. No matter how stark our differences, it would seem we all share a connection to the wolf." He nodded matter-of-factly at Yusuf's jersey before turning to Rowan.

"As for you, Ms. Dobrzynski, you said you were an artist?"

The girl nodded without a word.

"So then, would it be too bold of me to assume that you have used wolves as subject matter?"

"Not wolves," she said, pulling what appeared to be a sketchbook from her bag. She flipped through its pages for a moment before deciding on one to share. "*Werewolves*," she clarified, and the drawing she revealed could have been the cover art for one of Elijah's novels.

"Amazing," said Nicholas.

"Seriously," said Yusuf.

Rowan shoved the book back into her bag before any more compliments could be made, her face flushed a bright red.

"Jeez," Nora said, shaking her head. "Is there anyone here who's not insanely talented or literally famous?"

"I don't think we've seen anything yet," Nicholas said, and he directed the group's attention to a new vehicle approaching the pull-off.

A limousine.

The long, black car pulled up so that its rear door was directly across from the group, giving the crowd of guests a perfect view of their newest member. Emerging first as a pair of perfectly pedicured feet in platform heels, a young woman in an elegant gray dress stepped out with two matching suitcases in tow. Struggling for a moment with one of their extending handles, she paused to remove her sunglasses, at which point Nora gasped.

"Oh, my God," she said, one hand pressed to her chest. "That's Amelia Hyde!"

"What?" Rowan exclaimed, and her shock was matched by that of nearly the entire group.

"There's no way!" Yusuf added, though by the time the limousine was pulling away, its sole passenger having come that much closer, there was no longer any doubt.

"Um, hello," she said, nodding to the group once she'd come within proximity. "Is this the meet-up point for visitors of Valentina Wilmore?"

There were some small nods and grunts of approval, but nothing more. For a moment, it seemed the majority of the group had been starstruck.

The glib assessment must have sufficed, though, for Amelia's face quickly brightened. "Oh, good," she said, relief plain on her features. "For a moment there I was afraid I'd taken a wrong turn."

Her smile turned to a frown as she gazed from the group's attire to her own. "Oh, well, this is embarrassing. It seems I've overdressed."

"Not at all!" Damian exclaimed suddenly, the first to say something of substance. "You look absolutely stunning, my dear." He strode forward with a hand outstretched. "I am Dr. Damian Donegan, professor of anthropology at Breccan Augustus..."

Damian went on to introduce everyone in turn, Amelia smiling cordially at them all, though her eyes lit up at the last.

"Elijah?" she exclaimed. "What are you doing here?"

"Research for my next book, I suppose," he said with a shrug.

She laughed. "I suppose I'm doing the same. Gosh, it's so good to see you. How long has it been? Since we wrapped production on *The Wolfman of Winterville*?"

"Oh *that's* where I know you from!" Nicholas said suddenly, snapping his fingers with emphasis. "My girlfriend loves those werewolf movies." He turned to Elijah with an embarrassed look. "It's funny, I actually didn't know they were based on books."

"Most people don't," Elijah said with a shrug. "Though what even fewer people know is that the books are based on real life."

"Really?" Nora said, eyes wide.

"No," the author replied with a smirk, and his gaze drifted to the forest beyond. "Though after this weekend...maybe they could be."

Amelia's expression suddenly became deadly serious. Everyone's did. Her voice dropped to a level just above a whisper. "So, what exactly is this? A weekend with an actual werewolf?"

"Or something of the sort," Damian said, pulling on the lapels of his jacket. "Something tells me we'll be learning exactly what this weekend shall entail very soon. The instructions were to meet here at five o'clock, were they not?"

Assorted nods from the group.

"Well then, seeing as it is currently five of five," Damian continued, checking his watch, "I do believe our host should be arriving at any moment."

"Bingo," Nicholas said, pointing to the road again. New wheels could be heard crunching their way toward the pull-off, ones attached to something decidedly not limousine.

The vehicle that arrived was an interesting one, a kind of cross between a UTV and a short bus. The buggy was dark black in color, roofless and wall-less on all sides, and driven by a short man of middle age with beady eyes and a flat brim ball cap pulled real low. He careened the buggy toward the crowd of guests with frightening speed, coming to a grinding halt only inches from a flinching Damian.

Keeping his headlights on, the driver crawled out of the cab and stood before them so that his silhouette cast itself larger-than-life against the adjacent treeline. With his arms crossed and his lips pursed, he regarded the group with an eyebrow raised.

"You all guests of Ms. Wilmore?" he asked.

"Yes indeed, sir," Damian said, stepping forward once again. "My name is Dr. Damian Donegan, professor of anthropology at—"

"Yeah, yeah," the man said, cutting Damian off with a wave of his hand. He turned to the group and threw a thumb back at the cab. "If you're all with Ms. Wilmore, you can come on in."

And so they did, one by one until all but a single seat was filled, the likes of which seemed to trouble the driver. He did another head count, and his frown only grew deeper.

"What, only eight of you?" he asked, brow furrowed.

"That is correct, sir," Damian said from the frontmost seat. "Eight altogether. All good and accounted for."

The driver still didn't seem satisfied. Taking a small booklet from his back pocket, he ran his finger down a page, mumbling softly to himself as he read.

"No, see, that ain't right," he said, shaking his head. "Supposed to be *nine* of you, according to this." He turned the sheet around as if to prove it.

"Nine?" Damian echoed, doing a quick head count of his own. "Well, that can't be right. *Clearly* there are only eight of us."

The driver just shrugged his shoulders. "Nine's what they told me. Nine guests up to that old black mansion with the silver gate."

"Black mansion?" said Nora.

"Silver gate?" said Damian.

"S'what they told me," the driver said with a nod, but he shook his head right after. "Hell if I know what they're on about. Been driving around these woods for years, I have." He shook his head again. "Never seen no black mansion."

"Never *seen* it?" Damian exclaimed, sounding horrified. "Are you not an associate of Ms. Wilmore's?"

The driver cocked an eyebrow. "Are you?"

"Well, no, but—"

"With all due respect, sir," Amelia interjected, "how are you supposed to drive us to our destination if you don't know where it is?"

The driver flipped to a new page in his little booklet, turning it around to reveal a hastily scrawled map on one side.

"Got myself a guide," he said, and after a look over his shoulder, added in a hoarse whisper, "and a hundred dollars to *burn* the thing when I'm done."

"Burn it, you say?" Damian cried.

"Seems kind of extreme, no?" Yusuf asked.

"You saw the letter she sent," Nicholas said with a shrug. "Valentina Wilmore certainly has a flair for the dramatic. Though if what she says is true..." His eyes flashed warily to the driver, who just laughed.

"Don't you worry about spilling no beans to me. Whatever y'all got going on with Ms. Wilmore is between you and Ms. Wilmore." He leaned back in his seat and put his hands behind his head. "Frankly, I can't say I even care."

"Well that's all very well and good for *you*, sir," Damian said, growing increasingly flustered, "but I, for one, certainly *do* care. In fact, something I care very *deeply* about is being on time, something we all *won't* be if we don't get a move on!" He made a hurrying gesture to the steering wheel to which the driver merely blinked.

"I was told there'd be nine of you, and so we'll wait till there's nine of you."

Damian seemed about ready to explode at that, though was cooled by Nora's placing a hand at his shoulder.

"Well we can't just wait here all night," Yusuf said, eyes turned to the steadily dimming sky. "At some point…we might have to accept that maybe number nine isn't coming."

"Yes," Nora agreed with a nod. "Maybe they declined."

"Declined?" Elijah echoed. "An invite as tantalizing as Ms. Wilmore's?" He'd meant it as a joke, though the instant he said it, the author realized there was some truth to it as well. Something about that letter had been strangely compelling, had seemed almost impossible to ignore. It seemed Elijah was not alone in this feeling, for alongside the smiles, he spied small nods of agreement.

"Could be their car broke down," Rowan suggested.

"Could be they got lost," Amelia offered.

"Could be the poor guy walked the entire way," Nicholas said, and for the third time that evening, he drew the group's attention to the adjacent road, to where a new figure appeared to be approaching on foot.

At first, Elijah could only make out a purple shirt and a messy tuft of dark hair, though as the walker neared, he soon got a better picture.

The kid couldn't have been more than twenty-two, with olive skin, shaggy black hair, and a slow, shuffling gait. He wore a graphic purple t-shirt and black jeans, his hands shoved deep into the front pockets. Though the sun had already dipped well below the treeline, the boy seemed to squint for the brightness.

He came to the side of the buggy and was immediately greeted by Damian.

"Young man, might you be the ninth guest of Ms. Wilmore?"

The kid seemed to squint harder at this, tilting his head as if the professor had just asked him a complicated math question. It took him a moment, though eventually he replied.

"For the uh...werewolf thing?"

"The very same," Damian muttered, not so subtly side-eyeing the driver, though the shorter man seemed as indifferent as ever. "Now, tell me this: did you *walk* to this location?"

Eyes shifting from side to side, the kid slowly nodded.

"My dear boy, why?"

"It was only the last couple miles," he said with a shrug. "Had a taxi from the airport but I, uh...ran out of cash."

Elijah felt a sudden swell of sympathy for the boy. Never before then had it occurred to him that such a venture might prove a financial blow to a guest other than himself. Of course, no invitation was mandatory, and the boy could have easily refused, but then, Elijah recalled again the letter itself, and the thrall it had seemed to hold over him.

"I see, well, come aboard then," Damian was saying. "We're all waiting on you."

The young man climbed gingerly onto the bus, giving small nods here and there but mostly keeping his head down before slinking into the last unoccupied seat. It happened to be the one right across from Elijah.

"How's it going?" he said, offering a hand when the boy looked his way. "I'm Elijah."

"Julian," he said, giving a light shake. He met Elijah's eyes for a moment, though his gaze quickly fell away, retreated to his lap and to the details of the floorboards.

Elijah gave another nod, a small smile on his lips. The kid reminded him a bit of himself as a twenty-something, all clenched jaws and sweaty palms. So many thoughts in his head. So few words out of his mouth. He'd shaken most of his anxieties off by his thirties, had come out of his shell with more than a little help from his best-sellers. It had been a long road, and he was glad he'd traveled it, but it was kind of fun to think back too, to reminisce about the old days, those days when he and Julian might have been one in the same.

The young man wore a purple t-shirt with a cartoon wolf on its front, the familiar name *Willy Wolfgang's Pizzeria and Arcade* emblazoned below it, and in big white letters across the back: *STAFF*. Here laid another similarity, though Elijah grimaced at the thought. Whereas he could look back on most of his awkward youth with some nostalgic fondness, the minimum wage job was one part of his twenties he definitely didn't miss. It worked for Julian, though, and specifically in terms of his being the final link.

It seemed it was true then, it seemed all the guests were connected.

By *wolves*.

At the front of the buggy, the driver had just turned the keys in the ignition.

"Okay then," he said. "Now that everyone's accounted for, we can head out. Hold onto your hats though, yeah? Next stop, Wilmore Manor."

Chapter Two

The House

The drive to the manor was not long. Nor was it particularly short. Had she been asked to pinpoint its exact length, Rowan would have had no idea. Surprising, considering she'd been conscious for the entire ride, though admittedly, her mind had been elsewhere. And her eyes too.

Down in her lap, in the dimly lit pages of her sketchbook, Yusuf Miller was taking shape.

Had anyone asked her, she would have claimed she was studying, drawing from life as a way to pass the time and hone her ever-developing skills. Yes, one of these reasons or all she would have said, and all were technically the truth...though none were the *whole* truth. The whole truth was that drawing Yusuf meant keeping her eyes on him. And since they'd boarded the same flight at the airport together, Rowan had been unable to do anything but.

She'd misjudged him on the train ride. Had initially pegged him as a typical jock type, brutish and uncaring. Shallow and one-dimensional. She'd let her mind fill with all the worst assumptions, and then more when she'd found out he was a star quarterback. It had seemed perfect in the worst possible way. There was no way someone so muscular and good-looking could not have a giant-sized ego to match. No way someone so successful and high up in the societal pecking order could be so down-to-earth in a conversation. Only...Yusuf *had* been, and for the entirety of the plane ride where fate had sat them right next to each other.

Not only had he turned Rowan's worst assumptions on their head, but he'd proceeded to subvert them until it had felt like Rowan's own head was spinning. Yusuf hadn't been a self-centered oaf. He'd been smart and courteous, humble and funny. An environmentalism major with dreams and depth that seemed only to expand the more they'd talked. So impressive was he, that Rowan's contempt had actually turned to nerves after a while, and to feelings of inadequacy. She'd found herself talking less and less the more they'd conversed, slowly clamming up as she realized how much she liked him. What was a girl like her doing talking to a guy like him anyway? Maybe it wasn't that she was out of *his* league...but that he was out of *hers*.

He'd liked her drawings though, and so that was something.

She was just fixing the shading around his hair when the trees broke, erasing a greater shade as the path the buggy was on opened up into a clearing. Though it was not just any clearing; it was an entire estate. A grassy, pedicured landscape some two or three acres, and all of it tucked away in the middle of the Adirondack wilderness. It was a woodland oasis, something from the pages of a fairytale, and in the center of it all, Wilmore Manor.

Somewhere behind her, the flash of Nicholas's camera brought Rowan back to reality, though it was admittedly a strange one.

"My word!" Damian said, clearly awestruck.

"It's magnificent!" Amelia added, clearly the same

All around were comments and sounds of a similar sort. Even Proctor, that grim, silent gentleman in the cowboy hat, seemed somewhat captivated, though it was a captivation tinged by his ever-suspicious quality.

"Well, I'll be damned," the driver said as he crossed onto the gravel path from the dirt road they'd been on. "All these years I've been driving these roads, and not *once* have I seen this old place." He gave a weak shrug and shook his head. "Guess I must've missed it."

"Not sure how you could have," Nicholas said. "This place is *huge*."

It was. A two story, Victorian mansion, the place looked fit for a dutch or dutchess—for a few of them, maybe. Constructed almost entirely of brick and stone, the gray monotony was broken up only by a uniform set of dark shutters and window frames, and all of it beneath a pitch-black roof.

It was an intimidating look, the black, and especially on the spire which stood tall to one side, though Rowan loved it. It had a gothic and macabre aesthetic to it that reminded her of her art. And of herself too, she supposed.

If there was a single part of the manor she didn't care for, it had to be the great silver fence which surrounded it on all sides.

"Quite the fence," Nora said. "Who's she trying to keep out?"

"Buggies full of tourists?" asked Elijah.

"Werewolves?" asked Yusuf.

Damian harrumphed. "If either were the case, I fear Ms. Wilmore would have failed on both accounts. Look there," he said, pointing forward. "The gate opens before us!"

It was true. No sooner had the buggy rolled within spitting distance of the gate than did its large, silver frame begin to move, a doorway presenting itself within the great barrier.

They passed through it and Rowan felt a strange shiver run down her spine.

"All right, then," the driver said, easing the buggy to a stop. "End of the line. You all can make it from here, I reckon?"

"Indubitably," Damian said, rising from his seat first. "Thank you very much, and good day to you, sir."

He departed from the buggy and the rest followed. No sooner had the last guest stepped off than did the driver honk the horn twice, step on the gas, and peel away, back down the drive they came, going so fast that the gravel kicked up behind the rear wheels in dirty plumes.

"A rather *hasty* departure," Damian commented, watching the fading silhouette of the buggy with an eyebrow raised.

"Perhaps he had another werewolf tour to get to," Elijah said.

"Or maybe he was making sure he beat the gate." Nicholas nodded to the silver doors they'd entered through, silver doors that were now gliding shut. They did so with a loud, metallic clang, the likes of which made Rowan jump.

"Is it just me," she began, staring warily at those silver walls, "or is something about that fence creepy as hell?"

"It's not just you," Yusuf agreed, frowning. "There's definitely something unnerving about it."

"No escape now," Amelia sang, a cryptic look on her face, though a second later, upon a few concerned looks from the others, she laughed. "Just kidding! I'm sure it opens from this side too."

"Well, of course it does!" Damian said, looking positively disturbed. "You young people and your anxieties." He shook his head. "It is just a gate." He spoke the words with confidence, though Rowan thought she caught a shred of doubt in his eye. A shred of fear.

"Shall we go in, then?" Nora offered, grabbing her suitcase and beckoning the group toward the front steps. "I think we've kept our host waiting long enough."

She started up the long driveway and the rest followed, until they were all crowded on the large front porch, on the doorstep of Wilmore Manor.

Nicholas was the first to knock, lightly at first, and then harder. Five solid raps with an old-style knocker, this one a dark black thing sculpted like a rose.

After a third, unsuccessful try, he stepped away, brow furrowed.

"Maybe she's not home," he said with a shrug.

"Not home?" asked Yusuf.

"On the night of an engagement she organized?" asked Nora.

"I've forgotten worse," Elijah said with a shrug.

"Preposterous!" Damian cried, seeming to have grown even more impatient. "Step aside, will you?" he said, muscling his way to the front. "Allow me to try."

Rather than use the knocker, Damian pounded directly on the door itself, three bangs powerful enough to make Rowan blink on each repetition, and on the last, for the door to move too.

With an eerie squeal, the large oak door slowly opened, revealing, by an ever-widening crevice, warm light from within the black mansion.

"Jesus, man," Nicholas said, rounding on Damian. "You didn't have to bust the damn thing in!"

"I did no such thing!" Damian cried defensively. "It was already open! I swear it was! All I did was give it a *push*!"

"Is that what you call that? A *push*?"

"Oh, hush both of you," Nora hissed, grabbing both men by their sleeves. "We've already arrived late and broken the poor woman's door down. The last thing we need is to be found bickering on her doorstep!"

This quieted the two men, and the rest of the group as well. For a long moment, they all just stood there, waiting patiently before the half-open mansion. Rowan craned her neck to get a better look inside. She couldn't see much, but it seemed the manor was just as decadent and impressive on the inside as it was on the outside. And the longer the door stood open, the more a delicious aroma seemed to waft out from within, tickling Rowan's nostrils and making her stomach grumble with a newly perceived hunger.

"Mm," Amelia said, lifting her nose to the air. "What is that smell?"

"Clams, I think," said Yusuf.

"And steak," Elijah added, dreamily.

"Did she say dinner would be served?" Rowan asked. She could feel her mouth watering already.

"Well, I should hope so," Damian said. "To host so many at this hour and not would just be uncivil." He shook his head ruefully. "No, I refuse to believe that someone of Ms. Wilmore's repute would be so distasteful. The foods we smell currently are most certainly for us, and I, for one, plan to *partake* in them." The professor made to step forward then, through the doorway and into the manor, but was stopped short by Nicholas.

"Whoa, dude! You're just gonna let yourself in?" he said, one hand on the professor's shoulder.

"Do you attest, Mr. Chau?"

"Well, it's just...we haven't been invited in yet."

Damian laughed. "Oh, what are we? *Vampires?*"

Nicholas frowned. "What?"

"Vampires, I said. Good God man, have you no knowledge of the creatures?"

At Nicholas and the group's collective confusion, the professor sighed.

"Common lore states that the vampire must be invited into a place before he or she can enter. Otherwise, they are constrained beyond."

"Um, I thought this trip was about meeting a werewolf," Amelia said, still looking confused.

"That it is, Ms. Hyde," Damian said, sighing again. "I was merely making a joke. One I fear landed about as well as mine commonly do among my undergraduates." The professor took a moment to rub his eyes before continuing.

"Either way, it matters not. Even if I *were* a vampire, I would face no challenge entering Ms. Wilmore's estate, for I have *already* been invited, as have we all." He pulled an envelope from his jacket just far enough so that the familiar red ink on its front could be read before tucking it away.

"So, Mr. Chau, while I appreciate your concern, I do believe that it is unwarranted. Why, Ms. Wilmore is likely in the dining room now, well out of earshot of the front door, singly enjoying a dinner meant for ten. Now, I don't know about you all, but I'd rather not keep her—*or my stomach*—waiting any longer!"

He gave a final nod, and with a forceful stride, crossed the threshold into the manor.

"He really did it," Nicholas said, shaking his head once the professor's form had fully disappeared within the mansion. "The crazy bastard just let himself in."

"Maybe he's right," Elijah said, stepping forward. "Maybe she *is* waiting for us."

"Don't tell me you're going too," Nicholas said, eyes wide.

"Not like it can hurt much now," the author said with a shrug. "Besides..." he brought a hand to his stomach, "...I'm hungry."

And with that, the second of the group stepped through as well, leaving just seven on the doorstep, though not for long. Soon enough, Amelia, Julian, and Nora stepped through too. Even Nicholas eventually conceded, shaking his head as he seemed to chase the others in rather than enter of his own volition. In the end, it came down to the three of them: Rowan, Yusuf, and Proctor.

Yusuf spoke first. "Well, what do you think?" he asked, looking from Rowan to the door, an eyebrow raised. "You going in?"

"No choice now, right?" She gave a shrug. "You?"

"I think I will," he said with a nod. "Already came this far." He turned to the man behind him. "How about you, Proctor? You going in too?"

The rugged man did not speak for a moment, and did not turn toward Yusuf or Rowan at all. His gaze was fixed upon the mansion itself, those dark eyes ever-suspicious beneath the shade of his brim.

He turned his nose to the air, took a couple whiffs of the steadily building aroma before turning to spit over the railing, shake his head with a frown.

"Something about this don't smell right," he said, voice dry as a bone. He shook his head again. "Don't smell right at all."

"To each his own," Yusuf said with a shrug. "Me personally, I think it smells great." He turned back to Rowan and nodded to the door. "Shall we?"

"Sure," Rowan said with a smile, trying to ignore the butterflies that had just leapt to life in her stomach. She and Yusuf then stepped through the doorway, leaving Proctor alone on the porch.

The hunter stayed out there a long time, though eventually even he relented, stepped over the threshold and into the manor. He shut the door behind him, and then the porch was empty. The guests had arrived.

***

As soon as the man in the cowboy hat shut the door, Julian felt his heart rate spike. He should have never agreed to this. Should have just kept his head down—should have kept it in the much larger head of Willy Wolfgang. Did he hate entertaining snotty kids and clueless parents? Of course he did. But at least he knew what he was getting into with that. At least that was his element, as sad as it was to admit.

He should have never agreed to this. Should have tossed out that letter just as soon as he'd gotten it. Should have fed it to the ticket taker, even, let that purple machine mince it into a million little unrecognizable pieces. Yeah, that's what he should've done.

But there'd just been something about it, hadn't there?

Something about that letter that had been enticing, had been impossible to ignore. Impossible to *resist*. There'd been something about it, yeah. Something enough to make him spend the last of his cash on a plane ticket to nowhere New York state and hole himself up in a mansion with a bunch of strangers for an impromptu weekend vacation.

It'll be worth it, whispered the little voice in his head.

That letter, it had offered him an opportunity. A discovery. A change, if nothing else. At the time, reading it in half a wolf suit ripe with the smell of his own must, that last bit had been enough. At the time, he'd have done anything to get as far away from that stinking arcade and pizzeria as possible. Now that he had, though, now that he was neck-deep in unfamiliar territory, a good hundred miles from the nearest Willy Wolfgang's in any direction, a part of him wished he'd never left.

The place, at least, was gorgeous. Better than anything Julian had ever seen, even in movies. The others were certainly impressed. This lot of actors and authors and doctors and scholars—the types of people who likely didn't dwell in the backseat of a gutted old sedan—and even they were impressed. Julian figured that must have said something. The oldest one, the professor, was probably the most impressed of all.

"My word!" he said. "The place is fabulous!"

They stood in a sort of atrium, a large, high-ceilinged room that seemed to lead off into every other space of the house. To his right, Julian spied what looked to be a parlor. To his left, an entertainment center—or so the pool and foosball tables led him to believe. Two staircases stood to his front, an elegant, winding pair which met at an open, second story balcony. Below this, and between the stairs, was a long hallway leading to the back half of the house, and it was from here where the delicious smell of food seemed to waft.

"So fabulous!" Amelia said, a hand to her forehead, seemingly overcome. "This place is a dream!"

All around, there were comments and sounds of a similar nature, and the group quickly began to disperse, slowly but inextricably pulled in every direction either by sight or smell. Julian had just taken a step toward that frontward hallway himself, the grumbling of a growing hunger ever apparent in his stomach, when the one with the camera spoke.

"Now hold on everyone," he said, a sobering command to his voice. Beside the rugged man in the hat, he had been the only one to not step further than a few feet into the manor. "We've already let ourselves in. Maybe we should wait a moment before letting ourselves further."

"A shrewd idea, Mr. Chau," said Damian, immediately retreating from where he'd strayed into the parlor. He seemed to laugh at himself. "Look at me just wandering about. Look at all of us!" he said, gesturing to the rest. "It would seem Ms. Wilmore's estate is not without it's *witchery*."

There were some nods of agreement at this, and a few more embarrassed backsteps.

"Either that, or we're all just hungry," Yusuf said, to more nods.

"I'm so hungry I could eat a horse," Elijah joked, and Amelia gasped.

"A horse? Are you serious?" she asked, seeming genuinely dismayed.

When Elijah only smiled, Nora patted the actress on the shoulder. "It's just an expression, darling. I'm sure Mr. Vaughn here wouldn't *actually* eat a horse."

"Well, I would hope not," Amelia said, shaking her head vehemently. "They're so pretty." She seemed to smile dreamily at the thought, her previous horror all but forgotten, leaving Julian and a few others to regard each other with slight confusion.

"Right...well, enough dilly-dally," the professor said, clasping his hands together. "Allow us to make ourselves known." He turned on his heel then, faced the manor frontward and in a loud, booming voice, called:

"Hello? Hello, Ms. Wilmore? It is Dr. Damian Donegan and the rest of your invited company for the weekend! Are you there, Ms. Wilmore? Hello?"

After the last echoes of his voice had rung out and only silence remained, Damian turned back to the group, his lips pursed, his eyebrows furrowed.

"Well, that's odd," he said, concerned. "Do you think she heard me?"

"Not sure how she couldn't have," said the girl dressed in all black, rubbing an earlobe. She'd had the misfortune of standing right next to the professor when he'd made his call.

"It's a big house," Elijah said, looking up toward the ceiling. "Maybe she didn't."

"Should we try and find her?" Nora asked.

"And intrude even further!?" Nicholas cried, now thoroughly exasperated.

"Now, now, Mr. Chau, we *were* invited."

"I say we take a look," Julian said suddenly, more to quiet the debate than anything. That professor's voice had begun to grate on him. When he found that the group's eyes had fallen on him, however, all of them expectant of justification, he regretted it.

"I mean, we've already broken and entered," he said with a shrug. "What more harm can we do?"

"Kid's got a point," Elijah said, and he gave an amicable nod Julian didn't return.

"I, too, concur with the young man's decision," Damian agreed, already moving forward. "Shall we start with the dining room?"

And so with varying levels of eagerness, the party followed the professor down the center hallway, toward the increasingly potent smell of food. The hall eventually emerged into a large dining room, and the food was found. Lots of it.

A table for ten had been set, the makings of a five course meal laying marvelously upon it. All of it recently prepared, all of it mouth-wateringly enticing.

"My word," Damian said, clutching the wall as he swooned dramatically. "It's beautiful."

"It's so much," said Yusuf.

"Ms. Wilmore cooked this all herself?" asked Rowan.

"Maybe she has a butler," said Nora. "Or a chef!"

"A butler and a chef...but no doorman?"

"Who needs one when your guests just kick it in?"

"Was that intended as a slight at me, Mr. Chau?"

"Whoever made it did so recently," Yusuf said, one hand hovering over the nearest dish. "This pasta's still hot."

"So then, where are they?"

No answer to this. Outside, Julian could hear a hard wind blowing.

"Hot food on the table, and yet no sign of who made it," Damian said, stroking his chin. "How mysterious."

"Ooh! Maybe she's hiding from us!" Amelia said, raising a finger. "Maybe she wants us to find her!"

"Don't be silly, dear girl," Damian said. "Why would someone invite guests to their home only to conceal themselves upon their arrival?"

"Maybe for the same reason they invited those guests in the first place?" Nicholas offered. "I mean, look at this place. Look at the letters we got. All things considered, Valentina Wilmore doesn't exactly fit the typical party host." He shook his head and let out a small laugh. "I can't believe I'm saying this, but maybe Amelia's right. Maybe she *is* hiding."

"Oh, God," Nora said with a laugh. "This is starting to sound like the premise of an Elijah Vaughn novel."

"Whoa there, partner," Elijah said with a grin. "I write horror. Leave mystery to the professionals."

"Whatever," Julian said, once again sick of all the talking. "Let's just find her." He found himself gazing longingly at a pepperoni and sausage pizza halfway down the table. "I'm hungry."

"Another fine request from the lad in purple!" Damian exclaimed, shooting Julian a smile he didn't return. "Let us begin the search for our elusive host. The quicker we find her, the quicker we might feast!" He brought a hand to his large stomach, and Julian thought he heard a quiet gurgle.

"Should we split up, then?" Yusuf asked, peeking around the next corner. There seemed to be even more rooms branching off from the dining hall than had the atrium.

"I believe that would be best, Mr. Miller," said Damian. "Each person to a room. I daresay the place has enough to go around. Dividing our efforts, we should be able to comb through them all quite efficiently.

"Sounds like a plan," Nora said, and with that, the group went their separate ways—each to a different room of the black manor, each to search for some sign of Valentina Wilmore.

***

Amelia chose the upstairs to investigate, and particularly the master bedroom. One of them, at least. There seemed to be a few on the second story. Unfortunately, her search for Ms. Wilmore came up empty, and this saddened her for a moment, though the luxuriousness of the room quickly roused her spirits. Now *here* was a place matching the tenor of her outfit.

But then...there was something off about it, wasn't there?

Though the surface shined with extravagance, modern glamor and artistic chic, it felt to Amelia's trained senses like little more than an artificial sheen. A thin curtain pulled just barely closed over something else...something hidden behind the manicured walls and regalia, something that pulsed with a darker, much older energy. It was an energy Amelia didn't like, and one that certainly did not mesh with her red carpet-ready dress and heels.

She pushed the ominous feeling from her mind, choosing instead to focus on more immediate problems. Once she'd done her sweep of the room and connecting bath, she began on her second motive for choosing a bedroom: changing into something cute.

It did not take her very long. She'd brought just the thing for casual, mystery vibes. Something like a character in an Elijah Vaughn novel might wear. What she realized too late, unfortunately, whilst trying to document the outfit for her socials, was that she'd chosen a bedroom without a mirror. There was not even one in the bathroom, which was strange, and for a moment, she debated changing rooms entirely. She'd already hung up the rest of her clothes in the closet, though, and so she eventually decided against it. There'd be other mirrors in the house, she figured. And other—hopefully better—energies, too.

***

Nora checked the kitchen, an illustrious, chrome-filled place that would have fit just as well in a five-star hotel or restaurant as it did in Wilmore Manor. There was space and supplies enough within it to house an entire cooking staff, though there were none to be found. Someone had been there recently, however. All around sat dirtied dishes and utensils, the various tools that had been used to create the masterpiece in the next room. Nora supposed it could have been the doing of a single person, though if Ms. Wilmore truly had been the one to cook dinner and prepare the table, where was she now?

***

Julian checked the atrium again, the entertainment room, and an upstairs bathroom. There'd been no sign of Ms. Wilmore in any of the three. No sign of anything, really, except the lavish stylings of an extravagant mansion. Most was of no interest to Julian, though the foosball table in the entertainment room caught his eye. The rotating players had shed their traditional blue and red colors for a curious gray versus black.

***

Yusuf was just finishing his check of one of the lower bedrooms when his phone dinged with a notification. It was a reminder he'd set for himself the day before he'd set off.

Home by Sunday night, it read.

He nodded to himself and pocketed the device. It was Friday now, and he had every intention of being home on time. Even if this engagement went long, if Ms. Wilmore had scheduled wrong and needed the party to stay a day more, he would politely refuse. He had obligations to meet, responsibilities to hold up. With the season drawing so near, and the semester too, he couldn't afford to take any chances. He'd be home by Monday night for practice, and by Sunday night, too. Sunday night for sure.

***

Nicholas was in one of the upstairs bedrooms when he caught a glimpse of that fence again, and the sight of it caused the hairs to rise on the back of his neck. It looked worse now somehow, though he supposed it always had. Driving up to it from the road, it had felt a little like approaching Alcatraz or some other super prison, floating down the River Styx and looking up at the black gates of the underworld.

Except they hadn't been black.

Seeing that big silver barrier for the first time, it had unnerved him, but then, at least he'd been outside of it, and at least there'd been a big, beautiful mansion beyond. Now that he was *inside* of it, and now that the only thing he could see beyond was the ever-darkening woods, he found there was little left to console him.

Viewing it through the lens of his camera, the sight was slightly less imposing, though the picture he took came out strange. In the display screen of his camera, the fence looked as silver as ever. Though as Nicholas looked upon the actual photo, all aglow in the shimmering luster of the setting sun, he swore that fence looked red.

***

There was no sign of anything in the pantry, though the sight of familiar brands of food and drink gave Rowan some ease. This place, this manor, it was like nothing she'd ever seen before. And while there was a certain wonder to it all, there was a certain menace to it as well. One that had begun to give her the creeps.

As she walked slowly through the food-filled room which seemed to be almost as big as her entire studio apartment, Rowan found herself rubbing the crystals she wore on a bracelet around her wrist. Oh, how grateful she was that she'd brought the ones she had. Garnet for protection and good luck, and hematite for courage, stability, and grounding. There may have been no scientific support for their benefits, but Rowan didn't care. There was no scientific support for a lot of things.

She'd been wearing the garnet and hematite combo a lot lately, so much so that those on her bracelet were likely due for a recharge. Luckily, there was a full moon coming up on Sunday. She'd just have to make it through the weekend first.

***

Elijah thought he'd been checking the last of the upstairs bedrooms when he stumbled upon the home office instead. Or at least, an office was how the room appeared on one side.

The other side was like a miniature library.

Floor to ceiling shelves lined the walls on one half of the room, ending only as those walls turned to windows, offering a spectacular view of the manor's backyard. Spectacular, that is, save for the silver monstrosity which outlined the perimeter. No, that fence was an eyesore and a half. Luckily, it was easy to ignore beside the rest of the view. Trees, mountain tips, and all, the thing was like a default screensaver or postcard made real. Elijah could definitely see himself writing here, and reading too, given the collection. Slinking his way along those tome-filled shelves, he couldn't help but take a few down and begin flipping through their pages. There may have been no sign of Valentina Wilmore up here, but Elijah didn't mind. At least for the moment, he'd found something better.

***

Damian had chosen the parlor to check, and when he'd found no sign of Ms. Wilmore, he'd felt entirely no shame in easing himself into one of the armchairs positioned by the hearth. He let out a sigh of relief as he sunk into its cushions. He was sixty-one this year, and feeling it every day. Damn his aching knees. Them and his back could make for a troublesome trio, though the cushions helped. After so long a day of such horrid seating, it felt good to finally have some comfort.

I'll just sit here a moment, he thought to himself. *Rest my eyes while the others continue the search.*

And this he did, though while he'd only intended to pause for a moment, within seconds of letting his eyelids droop, the old professor was fast asleep, and snoring loudly.

***

Proctor had been checking closets. Broom and storage, big and small. Nothing of note had turned up after the first three, and so as he closed in on the seventh, the hunter wasn't exactly holding his breath. The house surprised him, though. Rather than another walled off cubby, the last unopened door on the first story led down to a basement, the discovery of which succeeded in reviving some of his hopes.

Some of his hopes, and some of his apprehensions, too.

The big guy in the jersey came by just as Proctor found it, let go an appreciative whistle and hollered for the rest of the group.

"Y'all might want to come check this out!" he called. "Looks like Proctor's found something."

There was a scuttling of footsteps, some prompt, others delayed, though eventually everyone arrived, all of them peering down the dimly lit stairway like a herd of billy goats perched upon a cliff.

"Hello, Ms. Wilmore?" the professor called, loud as ever. "Hello, Ms. Wilmore! Are you down there?"

When no reply came, he shook his head in frustration. "Blasted mansions," he said. "Entirely too big to communicate in, I think."

"You think she's down there?" Nicholas asked, somewhere toward the back.

"She has to be," Yusuf answered, somewhere toward the front. "We've checked everywhere else, haven't we?"

There were some nods and grumbles of agreement at that, though still, no one moved. Eventually, the girl dressed all in black asked what everyone seemed to be thinking:

"Well, who's going first?"

Proctor stepped forward without a word. Seemed only right that he be the one to lead considering he'd been the one to make the discovery. If he had any reservations, it was only that leading meant turning his back on the rest of the group, a practice he was never fond of, and especially not with strangers.

Especially not with *these* strangers.

Seeing as little could be done in this particular instance, he resigned to taking extra care as he began his descent. Keeping a steady hand on the railing, Proctor started down the steep steps, and slowly but surely, the rest followed.

There was a light at the bottom of the stairs, a single bulb with a chain beside it. Grungy, by the standards of the rest of the house, though as far as basements went, Proctor had seen worse. He pulled the chain and squinted as black was replaced with harsh yellow and white. He blinked lightly at first, and then harder as he tried to make out what lay before him. And something did lay. When it finally registered, when his eyeballs adjusted and the details of the room finally came into focus, he just let out a sigh.

He knew there'd been something off about this place. He'd felt something wrong from the very beginning—had *smelled* it, even. And now here it was.

Stopping on the second to last step, halting the rest behind him, he turned to address the following procession. Vision blocked by the adjacent wall, they'd had yet to see what lay below.

"Found Ms. Wilmore," he said simply. "Those of you with weak stomachs might want to turn back."

"Turn back?" the professor echoed, him being the first in line following Proctor. "When our host is but three steps away? My good man, why?"

Proctor locked eyes with the old man, met them with a seriousness he hoped got the message across.

"It ain't pretty, doc."

"What do you mean, Proctor?" Yusuf urged, him the second in line. The look in his eye was guarded, enough to tell that he'd picked up on the hunter's tone. It seemed the others had too, for they had stopped their advance down the stairwell and were gazing at him with mixed faces of confusion and concern.

The professor, however, remained oblivious.

"Unbelievable!" he said, face turning pink. "Here we've spent how much time searching for our illustrious host, now to find her and not even *show* ourselves? I don't know how you were raised, Mr. Proctor, but in my opinion that is just *rude*. Plain rude. Now, if you'll excuse me..."

Proctor allowed him to muscle past.

"Ms. Wilmore!" he called as he descended the final steps. "Please excuse my tardiness and allow me to introduce myself. It is I, Dr. Damian Donegan, professor of anthropology at—"

The professor's words stopped short as he rounded the corner, as he finally caught sight of that which Proctor had moments before.

"Dr. Donegan?" Yusuf asked cautiously, still on the stairs, though he received no reply.

At the professor's prolonged silence, the rest of the group quickly filed down, none of them able to resist what had to be ballooning curiosities. Proctor didn't blame them. He figured there were a rare few things that could silence a man like Dr. Damian Donegan, and the scene in the basement of Wilmore Manor proved to be one of them.

There on the concrete floor, Valentina Wilmore lay dead, her throat torn open, the remains of a large, broken cage sitting empty beside her.

Chapter Three

The Body

"Oh, God," Rowan moaned. "Oh, God, there's so much *blood*."

There was. It pooled around the dead woman as if she'd fallen into a puddle, soaking her clothes and hair, separating into a million tiny tributaries as it ran to the ends of the room. As it ran all from the base of her throat.

Nicholas wasn't sure what possessed him to do it—maybe habit, maybe some higher power—but he took a picture. Used his camera to take a photograph of the dead woman with the flash on.

The football player, Yusuf, was on him in an instant. He grabbed Nicholas by his shirt collar and jerked him forward.

"The hell was that for?" he growled, eyes dark with anger, though there was fear there too. The same fear Nicholas felt.

"I don't know!" Nicholas yelled back, startled. He put both hands up, let the camera drop by the strap around his neck. "It was an accident," he lied. "I'm...I'm sorry."

After a moment more of glaring, Yusuf relented, let go of Nicholas's collar with a shove that sent the photographer back a step, made him think of his grade school bully. The quarterback might have been about a decade younger than Nicholas, but he was a whole lot bigger. Nicholas let the uneasy thought float to the back of his mind. As it stood, he had more important things to worry about.

They all did.

"What...what happened here?" Nora asked, palms at her cheeks, eyes wide with shock.

"Isn't it obvious?" Damian said, holding a handkerchief to his brow. "The poor woman has been murdered."

"Murdered?" Rowan cried, still visibly horrified. "But...but how? By *who*?"

"Look at the signs, my dear girl," he said, motioning to the empty cage. Its barred sides were dented and convex, its door cockeyed, still attached by but a single hinge. "Whatever Ms. Wilmore was holding, it seems it is held no longer."

The dark-haired girl's head whipped back, her eyes wider than ever.

"The *werewolf*," she whispered.

"I fear it could be," Damian said with a nod.

"Are you serious?" Nicholas said, still flustered. "But...there hasn't even been a full moon!" And not for a month either. In fact, he happened to know that the next would not occur until the coming Sunday. He'd been planning to take photos.

"It certainly *looks* like a wolf bite," Nora said, having knelt beside the deceased woman for a closer look.

Proctor let out a kind of bemused grunt. "That ain't no wolf."

Before anyone could ask what he meant, Yusuf was saying:

"Damn it, I can't even make a call." He was swiping at his phone screen in frustration. "Does anyone have service?"

No one did. It seemed they were far too deep in the Adirondack wilderness for that.

Beside him, Nicholas thought he heard Amelia mumbling something under her breath, something like *danger*, *danger*, *danger*, over and over and over again.

"All right everyone just calm down," Damian said, looking the least bit calm of any of them, though his voice was commanding, and his words spoke sense. "If there was something in that cage that got out and killed Ms. Wilmore, the real question we should be concerning ourselves with is where it is *now*."

"Here," Julian said. The young man had slunk into the corner of the room, was standing beside a lone cellar window, the glass of which had been shattered through.

"Oh, my God!" Nora cried. "It got out?"

"It or *they*, Ms. Inwood," Damian said ominously. "It just occurred to me that we should make no presumptions when it comes to the perpetrator of this horrible crime. While it could certainly have been the doing of a creature, I daresay it could just as well have been a man!"

"But what kind of man would do such a thing?" Nora asked, looking from the professor to the deceased Ms. Wilmore with horror.

"The kind that might do the same to us if we're not careful." His eyes swept carefully over the group and then widened.

"Hold on now, were there not *nine* of us in all?"

Nicholas did a head count and felt his heart drop as he came to the end.

There were only eight.

"I fear there is a member of our party missing," Damian said, a shadowy frown falling over his features.

"What?" Rowan said, looking around frantically. "Who?"

"The writer," Proctor said, regarding the group with a squinty glare.

"Elijah!" Nora gasped. "But...didn't he come down with us?"

"I didn't see him," Nicholas said, shaking his head.

"We have to find him," Yusuf said, already making for the stairs, though he was halted by Damian's hand at his shoulder.

"Take care, Mr. Miller. I agree that we must find him, and in a moment we will do so, though we must proceed henceforth as a unit. With an unknown killer on the loose, I fear anyone wandering about on their own invites grave danger."

"Good thinking," Yusuf said, nodding to the professor.

"Well, come on then!" Nora cried, taking the lead, and the rest followed, up the stairs to the first story, leaving the deceased Valentina Wilmore alone in the basement.

From there they went room by room, the entire crowd of them, together turning up nothing until arriving at the very last on the second floor, where they found a scene reminiscent of that which lay in the basement.

In a bookshelf-laden home office, Elijah Vaughn lay dead, an overturned book by his outstretched hand, the base of his throat torn savagely from his neck.

"Oh, God," Nora moaned. "Oh, *God*!"

"I think I'm going to be sick," Rowan said, and Nicholas could appreciate the sentiment. Here was a man who'd not thirty minutes prior been alive and well. A man who Nicholas had talked with and almost immediately taken a liking to. A man who now lay dead, murdered, and in a grisly manner at that.

"Not good," Amelia sang beside him, stretching out the vowels so that the words came out long and discordant. "Not very good."

"This is crazy," Yusuf said, clutching at his head as he paced the floor. "This is *crazy*."

Nicholas couldn't have agreed more. "We've gotta get out of here," he said. "Before whatever got them, gets *us.*"

And so they did. With quick, careful strides, the group made its way out of the mansion, constantly looking over their shoulders, vigilant of danger with every step. Thankfully, there was none to be found, though as they reached the front gate, the now eight party guests were met with another problem.

The gate would not open.

It could not. Where there should have been a handle or clasp at the center, there was nothing. Only more of those silver bars, as thick as they were uniform, and copious enough to stretch around the entire property.

Yusuf was the first to arrive at the gate, and he threw his hands up at its lacking appearance.

"What, no handle?"

"Preposterous," Damian declared. "There must be *some* kind opening mechanism." Though if there was, it did not make itself obvious.

"Well, there's a seam anyway," Rowan noted, pointing to the central slit where the gates were meant to bisect. "How did they open for us on the way in?"

"There seemed to be some kind of sensor," Damian said.

"And what, no sensor on the inside?"

"I doubt it," Nicholas said. "There isn't even a handle."

Yusuf was just shaking his head.

"What kind of door doesn't open from within?"

"The door to a cage," Amelia mumbled.

Nicholas found himself studying the actress, found himself comparing her to the face he knew from the screen. How many of her scary movies had he seen? How many times had he heard her scream? Watched her eyes go wide as she was confronted by some cinematic horror? Too many to count, probably. Enough that he could hear that scream in his head, could picture those pretty brown eyes gaping with terror. Only, they weren't doing that now. No, now her eyes were droopy, her mouth was a thin, trembling line, and the poor girl just looked despondent.

He supposed that was what real fear did. *Real* dread.

He wondered absently why the movies never showed that.

"Screw it," Yusuf said finally, stepping forward. He made like to force the gate open himself, though the second his hand touched one of the bars, he recoiled.

"Shit!" he exclaimed, jumping back.

"What?" Damian cried. "What is it?"

"The bars," he said, looking down at his palm. "They're...they're electrified."

"Electrified?" Damian repeated, narrowing his eyes and craning his neck forward. He seemed to listen for a moment. "But I hear no current!"

"You want to try?" Yusuf said, raising a hand. An ugly red welt had appeared where his skin had made contact. He used it to motion to the gate. "Be my guest."

"What kind of psycho electrifies the fence around their *house*?" Rowan asked.

"Someone who doesn't want anything getting out," Proctor spat.

"Anything?" Nora asked, looking up at those tall, silver spires. "Or any*one*?"

A cool wind fluttered through the trees then, chilling Nicholas to his core.

"Well then...what now?" Julian asked sheepishly, fists buried deep in his pockets.

"Now, young man, I'm afraid we find ourselves in peril. Grave peril." The professor turned back to the house, hands clasped behind him as he gazed upon Wilmore Manor.

"Trapped is what we are. Locked in with two dead and a killer among us. A killer whose identity remains unknown...and who has proven themselves to be *extremely* dangerous."

"Not good," Amelia said again, and Damian nodded.

The moon was rising now, the last of twilight giving way to the black of night. Nicholas shivered where he stood. Somewhere far away, a wolf was howling.

Chapter Four

The Plan

It wasn't much so far as plans went, though Nora supposed it was the best they had.

They'd gathered in the parlor, the lot of them spaced out between its various chairs and couches. A fire crackled in the hearth, and Nora found herself increasingly grateful for its light. She'd forgotten just how dark it got in the woods at night, so far away from the touch of civilization. Usually, she wouldn't have minded it, though tonight the shadows unnerved her, made her think of what might be lurking within them.

"It's not a perfect plan...though given our lack of options, I'm afraid it will have to do." The professor shook his head in frustration. "There simply *must* be a way to deactivate that fence from within. I refuse to believe otherwise!"

"Of course there's a way to deactivate it," Nicholas said, squinting at the atrium through his camera lens. "All we have to do is find the breaker box, flip a couple of switches, and it'll be bye-bye electric fence."

This had been the original plan of course, though when three thorough searches of the manor had yielded no such results, they'd been forced to adapt.

"I still don't see why we don't just keep looking," Yusuf said, clenching the arms of his chair so hard his knuckles were turning white. "If the breaker box isn't in the house, then it's gotta be out back. In some shed or outbuilding we haven't seen. It can't be far. If a few of us just went out and—"

"No," the professor commanded, his face stern. "No one leaves the house tonight. Not when it's this dark. And especially not when a killer might still be about."

"A killer being about is even more reason to leave," Yusuf protested, his voice as grim as Damian's. "Seeing as two murders have already taken place *within* these walls, *without* them might just be the safer place to be."

This seemed to hit a nerve, for a silence floated out over the group, one that might have lasted much longer had Nora not broken it.

"I'm sorry, Yusuf," she said, shaking her head at the quarterback, "but I have to agree with Damian on this one. That driver took us a long way from the pull-off spot. Off-road and downhill. Even if we did open the gate tonight, I'm not sure that any of us could find our way back to the cars."

"What about Proctor?" Yusuf said, turning to the man in the cowboy hat. "You said you were a hunter, didn't you? You could get us back there. Easy as following the tire tracks, right?"

"Sure," Proctor replied, his eyes barely slits beneath the brim of his hat. "But then, who said I'm ready to leave?"

If the rugged man's words struck the group as strange, no one said anything. He had a mysterious quality to him, that Proctor. Nora thought she'd noticed him eyeing Yusuf with a particularly suspicious expression, though it was hard to tell.

"I hear what you're saying about the killer," Nora continued, locking eyes with Yusuf. "But we searched this place three times over looking for that panel box. Whatever killed Elijah and Ms. Wilmore, it isn't here anymore."

Nora spoke the words confidently, though her mind whispered with doubt.

"If you say so," Yusuf said, shaking his head. He didn't seem remotely convinced, but then, no one did.

"So that's the plan, then?" Rowan asked from beside Yusuf. She'd fallen into her sketchbook for most of the conversation, though now she looked up. "Wait till morning?"

"That is correct, Ms. Dobrzynski," said Damian.

The girl in black nodded slowly. "Wait till morning," she repeated.

"Survive the night," Amelia whispered, and Rowan nodded at this too.

There was a short moment of silence, and then Nicholas cleared his throat loudly.

"Well then," he said, clasping his hands together. "Who's hungry?" he began to walk toward the dining room, though turned back when no one replied or followed.

"What?" he said. "If we're going to spend the night, we might as well do it on a full stomach."

Nora had lost her appetite at the sight of the first body, though the talk of food now sent her stomach grumbling all over again. The rest of the group must have felt the same, for they all filed into the dining room, casting wary glances at each other all the way.

Despite all of the food being cold, and much of it inedible after having sat out for so long, Ms. Wilmore's welcoming platter still proved delicious and abundant enough to satiate them all. So good was it, that some light conversation actually broke out over its course, the likes of which acted as a much needed distraction from the misfortunes at hand. Though the dark clouds hanging over her never fully dissipated, Nora was glad for at least a few moments wherein she could pretend this was just a regular weekend after all.

Unfortunately, any ounce of good cheer came to an abrupt end as Damian stood up from the head of the table and announced that he intended to turn in for the night.

Bedtime, Nora mused. How horrifying it became when one was already so deeply afraid.

"You don't mean to isolate yourself in one of the bedrooms?" she asked, more for herself than for Damian. The prospect of sleeping alone tonight, and in a foreign bed and bedroom no less, it was more than she could fathom.

Luckily, she was not alone.

"Heavens no," Damian said, shaking his head fiercely. "To sleep alone tonight—to separate ourselves when isolation has already killed—it would be akin to suicide. No, I believe it best that we stay together tonight. Sleep all in one room, with a rotating shift to keep watch."

This seemed a logical solution to Nora, and the group agreed. And so, gathering blankets and pillows from the numerous bedrooms, the parlor quickly turned from a distinguished gathering area to something reminiscent of a middle school sleepover.

Nora was the first to keep watch, waiting for an hour by the door while the others fell asleep—or while they tried to, anyway. Proctor was still up when it came time for him to relieve her, and it looked as if the rugged hunter might stay awake the entire night. Those thin, suspicious eyes always watching, always thinking.

It took Nora a while to fall asleep herself, though eventually she did. She fought any lingering fear with the simple promise of tomorrow, with the knowledge that just a few hours lay between her and daylight. And once the day came, then she'd be gone, escaped from Wilmore Manor and its shadowy corners. She'd be back home and back at her clinic. Back to helping sick puppies and kittens.

Back by Sunday, too. Definitely back by Sunday.

Chapter Five

The Photograph

When Yusuf awoke the next morning, he half expected to find his throat torn out from under him. It wasn't, thankfully. Checking with his fingers, the skin on his neck felt as smooth and intact as ever. His left foot may have been asleep, and his back fostering a nasty crick, but his throat was in the clear.

His palm still burned, though.

He awoke to sunlight in his face, and though at first it was blinding, a few squints and eye rubs soon set him straight. He'd slept near the edge of the parlor, on a collection of pillows and comforters and window drapes, though the last had been accidental. Those curtains which lined the nearest window were long and thick and black as the manor's exterior. Black enough to block out the sun entirely, Yusuf guessed, were they to be pulled tight.

Must have thought they were more blanket in the night, got caught up.

He thought about pulling them closed again but decided against it, turned instead to where that sunlight was streaming to. He had yet to really take a look at the rest of the slumbering room, and for a moment, he feared he might turn around to a horror show—everyone's throat gouged but his, and the perpetrator grinning in the doorway, just waiting for him to notice.

Luckily, this was not the case. A quick scan revealed that everyone was safe, and all were accounted for.

All, he realized, but one.

"Where's Nicholas?" he said suddenly, and loudly, louder than he'd meant to. His volume was enough that a few were pulled from their slumber.

"Hm?" Damian moaned, still half asleep. And there were similar mutterings amidst the waking party.

Proctor was the first to truly come to his senses, and almost immediately. Within seconds of opening, the hunter's eyes were awake and alert. They jumped quickly from Yusuf to the rest of the room, and then to the clock.

"He was the last on watch," the hunter said, rising from the armchair he'd slept in. "Seven to eight." Proctor pointed to the time and Yusuf saw that it was eight now.

"Who is it?" Rowan asked, rubbing her eyes from a spot on the ground some feet from him.

"Nicholas," Yusuf repeated, trying to ignore the rising fear in his chest.

The photographer had probably just stepped out, he tried assuring himself. To use the bathroom or maybe even to take some pictures. That was what photographers did, right? Take pictures?

They take pictures at crime scenes too, thought some sullen part of him. *Of newly dead bodies.*

Yusuf did his best to rid his mind of the image.

"We need to find him," he said, directing his gaze at Proctor, and the hunter nodded.

Without another word, the two made for the exit, though Yusuf's wrist was caught at the threshold.

"Wait," Nora said, managing to get the word out between yawns. Though the vet's eyes were still puffy with sleep, her grip was like iron. "We go...together," she said, and the look in her eye was like iron too.

Yusuf relented.

"Okay," he said with a nod. "But we need to hurry."

It took a few more minutes to rouse the rest, and particularly the lethargic professor, though soon enough everyone was upright, their shoes were on and tied, and the group was together crossing into the atrium.

The idea to check the house again was raised, though Yusuf resisted.

"Something tells me that if he went anywhere, he went outside. Maybe to find the outbuilding and get a head start on getting us out of here."

"It's what I would do," Rowan agreed.

Nora nodded too. "Lead the way."

They went out the front door and circled around to the back, passing a side of the house where ivy had been allowed to grow up the exterior, the leafy greens cutting a sharp contrast against the inky blacks.

The backyard of Wilmore Manor was not exactly as picturesque as the long, rolling drive that was its front, though it was far from shabby. A sizable patio intersected the area directly behind the house, with space and chairs enough for a large table and fire pit too.

It was all very nice, though Yusuf barely noticed the details. His eyes were fixed on a large, barn-style shed some ways off, tucked in the corner nearly against the fence line. Its door was open, the square-shaped hole a black maw in the bright day.

"There," he said, and broadened his stride.

Yusuf's pace was quick, almost running, as he closed the distance, though it screeched to a halt as he made it within a few feet. He'd come close enough to detect something just inside the doorway. A pair of feet, toes pointed straight up.

His heart dropped.

Nicholas Chau lay just inside the outbuilding, his camera on his chest and his glasses askew, a shiny mess of entrails spilling from his throat.

"No," Yusuf breathed, and beside him, Rowan gasped. She began to sob, and Yusuf felt like he could do the same.

A swell of rage suddenly engulfing him, he charged forward, past the corpse of Nicholas and into the shed, hoping to catch the one responsible, though he found nothing. The barn was empty, as spick-and-span as the rest of the manor, and ever without a trace of the now three-time killer.

"Damn it!" he screamed, punching the nearest wall in frustration, though he immediately regretted it. What he'd thought was wood had actually been some kind of polymer substitute, hard as stone, and his hand lit up in pain, his knuckles skinned in three places.

"How do they keep doing this?" he demanded. "How do they keep getting away?"

He tried to straighten his fingers and winced as they refused. Keeping them clenched instead, he just shook his head. "Three times now they've struck. Three times and we still don't have a clue!"

"I wouldn't be so sure, Mr. Miller," said Damian, and he nodded to that which laid upon Nicholas's chest. "Mr. Chau's camera remains intact. Perhaps he managed to photograph his killer!"

The group's eyes fell in unison to the large camera below them. The thing was still intact all right. In fact, it remained in Nicholas's grip, clutched between his pale fingers like the sword of a dead king.

Nora was the one to retrieve it, carefully lifting it by the lens and removing the strap from Nicholas's neck.

She powered it on, and the group huddled around her.

"What does it show?" Damian asked, craning his neck to get a look at the small screen.

Yusuf could see about half of it from where he stood, though he trusted Nora to describe.

"The first picture is of the manor," she said. "From the outside. He must have taken it on the ride in."

Yusuf nodded. "And the next?"

"A picture of the front porch. There you are, Yusuf. Rowan and Elijah too."

Yusuf caught Rowan's eye and a shiver passed between them. To think that the author in the picture with them no longer drew breath, and the photographer neither...

"Let's keep going," he said, and Nora did.

There were a few more like the previous, simple shots of the manor and its guests, all of them perfectly ordinary—though threaded through with an unsettling subtext, a phantom tension that did not release until the sixth.

Rowan gasped as it came on, and Yusuf did not have to see the entire screen to know what it was. The bright red was horribly telling.

"This must be of the basement," Nora said slowly. "Of Valentina Wilmore's blood."

Yusuf did not blame her for quickly clicking away. He'd seen enough blood in the last twelve hours to last him a lifetime. He reckoned they all had.

"The next is of the dinner table," Nora said, commenting on the seventh photo. "And the one after that the outbuilding!"

"You were right, then," Rowan said, turning to Yusuf. "He must have left to look for the breaker box."

"And found something else," Yusuf said, frowning at the photographer's body. He turned back to Nora. "Is that the last picture?"

"It looks like there's one more," she said, clicking to it, and the instant she did, her eyes went wide.

"What?" Damian demanded, desperately craning to see. "What is it?"

"It's...it's..." Nora's eyes were still locked on the screen, the confusion and fear in them seeming to keep her from speech.

"What, Nora?" Yusuf said. "What is it?"

Her eyes turned to him then, and she turned the camera too, made it so that everyone could see the small display. A new image had taken over the screen, one a bit blurrier and low quality compared to the rest, though unmistakable all the same.

It showed a black-gloved hand wielding a kitchen knife. Slashing with it, or so it appeared. Murdering he who had snapped its picture.

Yusuf was still studying it, trying to get a sense of the details, when Damian suddenly jumped back, brought a hand to his mouth with a gasp.

"My God," he said, and pointed forward. "It was *her.*"

"Who?" Yusuf said, following the professor's finger. He turned to find that everyone else had suddenly taken a step back too. Not from him, but from the one beside him.

From Rowan.

"What are you talking about—?" he began, readying to whip around on the professor, but then he saw what they all did, and his blood went cold.

Rowan was looking down at her hands, the both of them outstretched and shaking. She was the only one wearing black gloves.

Chapter Six

The Gloves

"I don't care," Yusuf was saying. "It doesn't prove anything..." though Rowan could barely hear him. The fear was too loud in her head. Too abundant in the others' eyes as they watched her.

"Maybe not," boomed Damian. "Though I'd say it's *terribly* suspicious." The professor's eyes had grown cold, his posture stiff, like a large cat preparing to pounce. Had it been just the two of them, Rowan would have been afraid, though Yusuf stood between them.

He stood defending her.

And here you are, cowering behind him, spoke a critical voice in her head, and it was right. She hated herself for her immobility, though at the moment, it was all she could do to just steady her breathing.

The rest of the group stood to the outside, midway between Damian and Yusuf, still either too shocked or confused to have clearly picked a side. Though Rowan knew it was coming; it was only a matter of time. And if she continued cowering like she was, she had a feeling their decisions wouldn't be in her favor.

She was acting like she'd been caught. She was acting like she'd done it. She was acting *guilty*.

She needed to say something, *anything*. And she needed to do it fast.

"They're...they're fingerless," is what she finally managed. And she shoved her gloved-palms in the professor's direction.

"They're what?" Damian said, cocking an eyebrow.

"Fingerless!" she stressed, holding one hand of bare digits with another. "I...I always cut the fabric off at the knuckle...so I can still use my phone." Pausing to catch her breath, she nodded to the camera still clutched in Nora's hands. "Are they?"

Nodding to let Rowan know she understood, Nora examined the photo again, though her brow only furrowed.

"It's hard to tell," she said, turning the display again so that everyone could see. The image was so blurry, and the way the hand clutched the knife, only its gloved knuckles could truly be seen. Nora just shook her head. "They *could* be full gloves...but they could also be fingerless."

It was true. Even Rowan had to admit it. Her gloves being what they were didn't clear her whatsoever, though speaking up seemed to have done something nonetheless, seemed to have tipped the group's opinion ever so slightly in her favor. Nora especially.

"I don't think it was her," she said, stepping forward, positioning herself beside Yusuf. "Or at least, we can't prove it with this." She held up the camera. "Who's to say the killer didn't take this photo themselves to frame her?"

"Exactly," Yusuf said, raising a finger to the camera. "Innocent until proven guilty, right? And this doesn't prove anything." He turned back and gave Rowan a nod that made her heart swell. It swelled for both of them, actually.

And then, suddenly, Julian stepped forward too, positioned himself so that there now stood three between Rowan the accused and Damian the accuser. The quiet, scraggly-haired boy didn't say anything at first, though when expectant eyes and faces lingered, he merely shrugged.

"I don't know," he said, hands ever-stuffed in the front pockets of his jeans. "I feel like anybody could just put on a glove, right?"

It wasn't the flashiest of espousals, though Rowan's heart swelled for him too.

Only Proctor and Amelia remained undecided, the hunter's eyes as hooded with suspicion as ever, the actress blank-faced and mumbling incoherently under her breath, seemingly in her own world.

"Proof or not, something needs to be done," Damian said, still eyeing Rowan with mistrust. "I'm afraid that Ms. Dobrzynski's implication—be it definite or not—has still unearthed a certain disturbing possibility. One that, until this very moment, has yet to have been considered."

"What's that?" asked Yusuf.

"Until now, we have assumed these murders the acts of an outsider, of some third party unknown to us all. What we have failed to consider, then, is the possibility that the killer is much more known than we think, and closer too. Indeed, what we have failed to consider is that the killer could be one of our own."

The silence that fell over the party then was deadly, and Rowan shivered.

One of our own? she thought, and the idea was enough to send the hairs on the back of her neck standing. She didn't believe it. She *couldn't* believe it.

"But...why?" she said suddenly, shaking her head. "Why would one of *us* be killing the others? Why would one of *us* have killed Ms. Wilmore?"

"Why indeed, Ms. Dobrzynski," Damian said, still eyeing her with suspicion. "Why indeed."

"It would explain why we haven't found anyone else on the estate," Nora said, eyes shifting nervously around the group.

"And why those 'wolf bites' look so sloppy," Proctor said, nodding to Nicholas's throat, and he let out a dry chuckle.

"What, you knew from the beginning?" Yusuf said, rounding on him.

"Knew it wasn't no werewolf responsible," the hunter said, punctuating his words with a wad of spit to the ground.

Damian scoffed, blinking rapidly. "And are there any *other* observations you'd like to share? Preferably *before* another one of us is killed?"

Proctor shot Damian a deadly look at this, and though the professor may have stood a head taller than the hunter, there was something about the rugged cowboy that Rowan supposed would have made anyone falter.

"Do you?" Nora urged, addressing the hunter with delicacy. "If we're going to get out of this alive, we need to know."

After a long moment of silence, Proctor just shook his head. "All I know is there's something strange going on here. Something we're not getting yet." His eyes shifted slowly between everyone. "Though we'd best figure it out soon."

"Doomed," Amelia whispered, standing apart from the rest. She was holding her arms across her chest and rocking back-and-forth, wide eyes streaked with tears. "*Doomed.*"

"Not yet," Nora said, going to the actress's side. She wrapped her in a gentle embrace, though Amelia did not seem remotely comforted, or even aware. To Rowan, she seemed somewhere far away.

"It's going to be all right," Nora said, to Amelia and to everyone. "We think Nicholas came out here looking for the breaker box, right? Did he find it?"

Yusuf was the first to step further into the shed, and Rowan followed. There was a collection of outdoor tools and power equipment stored within, the likes of which Rowan might have found in her father's shed back home. The electrical panel was new, though. The metallic box sat upon the back wall like a beacon of hope. The Holy Grail shining out from within a black crypt.

"Yes!" Rowan cried, racing forward immediately, though her elation was cut short as she opened the small door and discovered what was inside. Or rather, what wasn't.

Each breaker switch was labeled with a corresponding circuit as scrawled upon a white piece of tape. Though while the labels listed everything from *Bathroom #3* to *Backyard Sprinklers*, there was nothing denoting power to an electric fence, or even to the gate.

"How odd," Damian said, examining the board for himself. "It would appear there is no circuit for the fence." He turned to Yusuf. "Are you quite sure it was electrified, Mr. Miller?"

"Of course it is!" Rowan said, rounding on the professor. "You saw the burn on his hand!" She'd meant to defend Yusuf as he'd defended her, though when she caught the quarterback's eye, she thought he looked more nervous than grateful.

"It's gotta be one of these," he said, still studying the breakers. "There's a few not labeled...and there's a chance one of these controls the fence along with something else—"

"So we shut 'em all off," Proctor said, leaning forward to deactivate the master switch. He did this in a fluid motion, though his eyes bored into Yusuf the entire time, watching him.

Rowan was watching him too. If she thought she'd seen fear in his eyes, it was gone in a second.

"Good idea," he said, nodding to Proctor. He then turned and began making for the door. "Let's go check it out."

And so they did.

***

When they arrived at the front gate again, no one was quick to jump forward, Yusuf least of all. Raising a hesitant hand toward the silver spires, he eventually let it fall. He shook his head and turned to face the group.

"I'm sorry," he said, head hanging low. "It's just,"—his eyes met Rowan's, then fell again, down to his palm—"it really burned last time." He shook his head again. "I don't think I can do it."

"That's totally okay," Rowan said, stepping forward. "I can—"

But someone beat her to it.

Quick footsteps behind made her turn, and just in time to avoid being trampled. Amelia had sprinted forward suddenly, had begun making for the gate, her eyes wide and crazed.

"Wait!" Damian called, trying to stop her, though the actress was determined, and quicker than she looked.

There was something unhinged about the way she ran forth, something raw and animalistic and rooted in terror. "Leave!" she screamed as she ran. "We need to *leave*!"

She threw herself upon the gate, wrapped her arms around those great silver bars, and then the real screaming began.

"*Aaaaaiiieeeeee!*" she bellowed, and it was like watching a horror movie come to life. Only Rowan thought she'd never heard a shriek so horribly real, so horribly in pain.

And yet, wasn't there something familiar about it?

She realized she could hear something alongside the screaming. Not the crackling pop of electricity, exactly, though it was similar. The sound Rowan heard was more like a sizzling, the steamy hiss a slab of meat makes when it first touches down on a skillet.

It wasn't until she began to smell it that Rowan realized just how accurate this metaphor was, though she probably should have sooner. Amelia's screams should have made it obvious. The gate was burning her, Rowan realized, cooking her like a slab of meat herself.

Nora and Yusuf were the first to act. They leapt forward to haul Amelia back, though the actress held fast. She seemed to be clinging to those silver bars, bucking against them despite their immobility, trying to break them despite how they burned her. She tried squeezing her head through one of the gaps, and Rowan watched in horror as her hair began to smoke.

"You need to let go!" Yusuf said, pulling at Amelia's shoulders and Nora her hips, though the actress still wouldn't budge.

"*Leave!*" she shrieked again, kicking and elbowing backward, one of each catching Yusuf and Nora both. The minute they'd detached, Amelia began to climb, began to scale the fence like an escaping convict. And the speed with which she did so truly *was* animalistic.

"What the *devil*?" Damian said, looking up in shock, and Rowan gaped with him.

The actress was fast. Insanely fast. And strong too, strong enough to summit the twelve-foot fence in seconds, and to withstand the pain all the while. Had she not wasted so much time at the base, had she tried immediately to climb rather than attempting to push and pull her way through first, she might have even made it. Though she hadn't, and while a person's pain tolerance only ebbs over time, heat flows.

She was just teetering over the top when she burst into flames. All at once she did. Like the head of a match that's been struck against its box, like a puddle of gas that's just caught light. Just, *poof*.

And then the screams. And then the *howling*.

She fell to the other side in a thrashing ball of fire, hit the ground with a heavy thud, and then continued to thrash, only weaker. Rowan had heard something snap when the actress landed. Whatever it was, though, it hadn't killed her, for she continued to scream, and she continued to burn.

Eventually, both things subsided, the screams first, and then the flames. What was left when it was done, what was left of Amelia Hyde, the once beautiful actress, was something just barely recognizable as human: a skeletal corpse charred black. It lay smoldering beyond those silver bars, its scorched limbs smoky and distorted.

In the end, Rowan supposed the actress had gotten what she'd wanted. She'd left Wilmore Manor. Though it had cost her everything.

Chapter Seven

The Flare

It was a few minutes before anything was said. A few minutes before the ambient hiss of the burned up actress finally ceased its sizzle. Even then, Julian could still see the charred parts of her skin crumbling, the whites of her teeth peeking out from within a black-burnt maw.

He wasn't exactly sure what he'd just seen, and Rowan was the first to put his own question to words.

"What...*was* that?" she asked, staring wide-eyed at the deceased actress, and at the fence too, he noticed.

That silver fence.

"I'll tell you what it was," Damian said, frowning at the newest corpse with more disgust than pity. "That was our killer killing *herself*."

"What?" Yusuf said, rounding on the professor. "Amelia? You can't be serious!"

"Deadly, Mr. Miller."

Nora was shaking her head too.

"No, no, no. That poor girl?" She shook her head some more. "It doesn't make sense!"

"Oh, but it does, Ms. Inwood," Damian countered. "Perfect sense, actually."

"But...but how?" Rowan asked, still watching Amelia's smoldering remains, though she quickly turned her eyes to the professor. Unlike his, hers were ripe with sorrow. "You saw her mental state. She didn't...she didn't seem *well*."

"Which is my point exactly, Ms. Dobrzynski. The woman was *unwell*. Deranged, by the looks of it. And possessing of both the incredible strength and speed necessary to carry out such grisly murders as we've seen." The professor nodded to the twelve-foot fence the actress had scaled, and even Julian had to admit he had a point.

She'd been quick all right. Almost inhumanly so.

"Given her net worth," Damian continued, "I wouldn't be surprised if this entire estate belonged to Ms. Amelia Hyde."

"What?" Nora said. "But what about Ms. Wilmore?"

Damian just shrugged. "For all we know she could have been a character. A sham. Another pawn in the actress's twisted game." His face turned grim. "She certainly fell victim to it in the end."

Now Yusuf was shaking his head. He even laughed, though it was without mirth. "Nah man, that's crazy."

"Is it?" the professor asked. "Because I don't think so, Mr. Miller. Tell me, what do we really know about the famous Amelia Hyde? What did we *think* we knew? That she was America's sweetheart? That we loved her in all those werewolf movies?" He shook his head. "It is but glitter, and with no gold underneath, I fear. The truth is, we didn't know a single thing about the *real* Amelia Hyde. Sure, she may not have *seemed* like a killer, but the woman was an actress for God's sake! A liar by trade!"

"It still doesn't make sense," Nora said. "If it's like you say, and she really did plan to kill us...why stop?" Her eyes turned to the pile of charred limbs beyond the fence. "Why kill herself?"

"To find logic in the actions of a madwoman is to go mad yourself, Ms. Inwood. The woman was *unwell*," Damian repeated. "I'm afraid that is all there is to it."

"Unwell, well," Rowan said absently. Her eyes had returned to Amelia. "After what we've seen...can any of us really claim either? Can any of us really know?"

A silence fell over the group at this, one Julian could feel in the pit of his stomach. He certainly didn't feel well; he hadn't since he'd gotten here. Something told him it was only going to get worse.

"Doubt me if you will," Damian said, drawing his hands behind his back and rising once to his toes. "If nothing else, the logistics certainly support me."

"And what logistics are those?" asked Nora.

"Why, the killings themselves, of course." He nodded as if agreeing with himself before continuing. "In each incident—the murders of Ms. Wilmore, Mr. Vaughn, and Mr. Chau—the victim was isolated. Alone but for the one who killed them. And who else was isolated at all three of those times? Removed from the group without alibi? Why, none other than Ms. Hyde."

"Plus everybody else," Yusuf said. "The same could be said for any one of us."

"What? No—" Damian began, though Nora cut him off.

"He's right," she said. "None of us have an alibi. I could just as easily have killed Elijah while we were all split up during the search, and again with Nicholas when everyone else was asleep. The same goes for Ms. Wilmore. Who's to say the two of *us* didn't have a secret trust fund?"

Looking like he wanted to protest, but sputtering every time he tried again to speak, the professor seemed to have finally had enough.

"Fine then!" he spat, crossing his arms tight over his chest. "Let us all continue to suspect one another! Let us agonize in anxiety whilst we await our impending doom! I *swear* I—!"

The professor was suddenly overtaken by a violent fit of coughs, the intensity of which seemed to strain him. By the time it was through, the anger had drained from his face, though Julian thought he looked older and grayer than ever.

"Sorry," he said, dabbing his brow with a handkerchief. "I'm sorry." Straightening slowly, he kept his eyes on the ground. "I fear the stress of it all has clouded my judgment. Forgive me."

He let go one last cough, and Julian was reminded that—as obtuse and abrasive as he was—the old professor was still human, and as susceptible to emotion as any of them. It made him like the old man a little more than he had, though it made his stomach churn too.

That bad feeling had not subsided.

"It's okay," Nora said. "After what we've seen today, we're all bound to be a little on edge."

Yusuf gave the professor a nod as well, though he shook his head soon after.

"Even if you are right, and Amelia was the killer, we've still got a pretty big problem." His eyes turned to the fence. "How the hell are we gonna get out of here?"

"I might have an idea," Julian said, raising a hand, though he quickly shoved it back into his pocket.

Something had caught his eye back in the tool shed, something that might just prove their best chance yet.

***

"A flare gun?" Nora asked, eyeing the red thing. She'd phrased it as a question, though that was exactly what it was. The scraggly-haired kid had caught sight of it back in the outbuilding. Proctor might have caught sight of it too, had he not been so focused on the kid in the jersey. Yusuf Miller, the D1 quarterback with the new burn on his throwing hand.

Yeah, he'd been watching Yusuf very carefully.

He was smiling now, had wrapped his arm around the much scrawnier boy.

"Great find, Julian!" He beheld the gun in both hands. "This might just be our ticket out of here!"

"Well don't just stand there!" the professor exclaimed, though he was smiling too. "Fire the thing!"

Yusuf did as he instructed, raised the gun to the sky and let fly a speedy ball of red fire. It went higher than Proctor had expected, flew to a height maybe double that of the nearest pine before arching back downward and fizzling into nothing. A flare like that *might* attract some attention, though Proctor wasn't hopeful.

Something told him Wilmore Manor wasn't done with them just yet.

Yusuf moved to fire the second flare, though Nora stopped him.

"Maybe we should wait until dark for the second," she said. "Spread them out so that more might see."

"Good idea," he said, and gave the gun back to Julian. He caught Proctor's eyes on the turn around, and unlike the professor, held his gaze for a beat.

There was something there all right. Something in the quarterback's eyes Proctor didn't like. Something cagey beneath the cool. Something *familiar*.

As far as Proctor's rankings went on possible suspects, the muscular quarterback had just jumped to *número uno*.

"How long will it take for someone to find us?" Rowan asked. She'd asked the group, though eyes instinctively jumped to Proctor. Eyes usually did, when it came to questions of the outdoor—or the unorthodox—variety.

The hunter merely shrugged. "Could be sooner, could be later."

The professor made a show of rolling his eyes. "Might you be able to *elaborate*?"

"Could be that driver of ours happens to be in the neighborhood, sees that signal and comes in the next five minutes." Proctor shrugged again. "Could be some hiker or fire lookout tower does the same, gets us help by tomorrow."

"And if no one sees it?" Rowan asked, eyes big.

"Then no one comes."

"Someone will," Yusuf said, placing a hand on the girl's shoulder. "They *have* to." He shook his head. "I can't afford to be trapped here for much longer. I have to be home—"

"By Sunday?" Proctor asked, eyeing the quarterback carefully.

"Preferably, yes," he said, once again holding the hunter's gaze. "I've got practice early Monday morning. And after the events of this weekend, I'd like to be able to get some rest in beforehand."

"Makes sense," Proctor said, though his eyes didn't change.

Rowan nodded quickly. "I'd also like to be home by Sunday night, if possible."

Proctor thought the girl looked nervous as she said it. Then again, she'd looked nervous all day, so it was hard to tell.

"I've got a plane to catch at noon," Nora added, and this prompted the professor to nod.

"I, too, have an engagement," he said, then turned to Proctor and Julian. "That leaves Mr. Proctor and Schultz. Do the two of you also have interests in getting home by tomorrow?"

"Work on Monday," Julian shrugged.

"Sure," Proctor said.

"Then it shall be so," the professor concluded. "Had it been only one or two of us in need of a timely return, I fear it may not have been enough. But all six of us?" He began to nod. "I say, those are odds to inform fate. To overturn it!"

Proctor thought the professor had a funny idea about fate, but he nodded along anyway. The truth was, the hunter also wanted to be home by Sunday. At the rate murders were happening at their current locale, he figured any sane person would. But then, Proctor had his own reasons too.

"I hope you're right," Nora said, watching the sky. A faint trail of smoke near where the flare had been fired could still be seen. "I just hope fate comes sooner rather than later."

"Same," Rowan said with a nod. "So then, what do we do now?"

"Now we wait, Ms. Dobrzynski. We wait, and we stay vigilant." The professor's tone dropped low, his eyes darting back-and-forth in a conspiratorial way.

"As has been made clear, a killer may still lurk among us. Whether within our group or outside it, we do not yet know, though until we do, I believe we would all do well to proceed with caution."

Silent nods from the rest of the group. Even from Proctor.

A killer still lurked all right. They lurked close.

"Right," Nora agreed, and turned toward the manor. "I don't know about you all, but I'm going back inside." She shivered despite the summer heat. "I can't stand to be out here anymore. Next to this fence, or next to..."

She trailed off, though Proctor figured they all knew what she meant. The stench of the charred actress was still thick in his nostrils.

As everyone else headed for the house, Proctor hung back. He wanted to check on something.

He went to the fence, to the place where Amelia had made contact, and to where her body now lay on the other side. He eyed the blackened corpse carefully. Had he had a feeling about her too? Some prickling sense that she hadn't been who she said she was? Proctor couldn't be sure, and he supposed it didn't matter now. His gaze lingered a moment longer on the actress's corpse and then left. She hadn't been the thing he'd wanted to check.

When he was sure the rest were far enough away that they wouldn't see, he raised his own hand to the barrier, and touched the tip of his finger to one of those silver bars.

It burned.

Looking down at the newly red spot on his finger, a grin came over his face, though there was no joy in it. And by the time he'd turned around, begun making his way back to the house, it was gone.

Something strange was going on here all right. Something *rotten*.

***

The group initially returned to the parlor, gathering together as they had before, though they did not remain long. The first order of business was to move the bodies. Neither Elijah nor Nicholas had been touched, and along with their worsening smell, the group agreed it felt wrong to just leave them where they had fallen. The basement was chosen as their temporary holding place, laid beside the deceased Valentina Wilmore and all three of them covered with spare sheets. It was not the neatest affair, though Damian accepted that it was the best they could currently do.

Of course, there was nothing they could do for Amelia, the poor soul. Killer or not, Damian thought the girl deserved better than to be left in a pile of her own soot. They'd make arrangements for her, and for all of them, once they got out, he decided.

If you get out, chanted a fearful voice in his head, though he did his best to ignore it. If he was going to survive whatever tricks this weekend still had in store, he'd need to keep his wits about him.

The second order of business was to look for clues. For the whereabouts of a certain kitchen knife and pair of black gloves, specifically. Except for a hole in the block where it had been taken, there was no sign of the knife, and the group had effectively turned the manor upside down in search of it. Little more progress was made on the glove front, though to no greater end. A pair of dark gray gloves had been discovered within Nora's suitcase—left there from a previous ski trip, she claimed—though it was decided that these no more proved her guilt than did Rowan's fingerless ones prove hers.

"Even if we found a bloody knife and pair of gloves beneath one of our pillows," Yusuf said, "it's not like we could trust it. The killer could have easily planted it there in an attempt to frame someone else."

"Indeed," Damian replied. "Though it disturbs me deeply that we have yet to locate them at all."

"Because that means the killer still has them?" Rowan asked, looking up nervously, as if the murderer might be crouched in the rafters.

Damian nodded. "That, and because the both of them must have a terrific hiding spot."

"And if they're hiding in plain sight?" Julian asked, eyes jumping warily between the various members of the group. "One thing we haven't checked yet is each other."

"He makes a good point," Yusuf said. "We should pat everyone down."

And so they did, though nothing more was found. It gave Damian some relief knowing that the murder weapon did not lay concealed up someone's sleeve, though the anxious part of him still stewed over just where else it could be.

And so it was that the group ultimately found themselves back in the parlor, six staring at the places where eight had slept the night before. There they existed in uncomfortable silence for a time, worried faces checked only by the occasional side-eye glare. Damian quickly grew tired of it, and rose from his lounge chair at the first grumble of his stomach.

"I don't know about the rest of you, but all of this searching has left me famished." He placed a hand on his stomach as it rumbled again. "Would anyone care to assist me in preparing lunch?"

"Are you sure that's a good idea?" Rowan asked, her eyes nervous. "I mean, to eat anything in the manor, or anything..."

She trailed off before finishing, though Damian thought he caught her meaning.

Or anything prepared by you?

"Your caution is understandable, Ms. Dobrzynski. Understandable, though unnecessary, I think. We all ate dinner last night, did we not? Food prepared in this very house?"

Small nods around the room.

"And are we not all still standing?"

"Not all of us," Proctor said. He was gazing at the spot where Nicholas had slept the night before, and at the spot a few feet away where Amelia had too.

"Er, right," Damian stammered, cursing his choice of words. "What I mean to say is that no food or drink has yet harmed us, nor any poisonous agent within them. I say, if there's one thing we know about our killer, it is that they are of a particularly *savage* kind. The kind that prefers to gore their victims as opposed to employing more indirect methods—the kind that wants to *feel* it." He paused to let a shiver pass through him before shaking his head. "No, our killer is not one for poison. For them, I suspect such a means of murder is too impersonal. Too easy. Too...*neat*."

"You seem to have put a lot of thought into this," Yusuf said, eyeing him crossly.

"And who wouldn't, Mr. Miller?" Damian said, eyeing him back. "In a game of cat and mouse, the roles are oft decided by who shows the bigger teeth."

"And if the cat turns out to be a wolf?" Rowan asked.

"Then I should care even less to be the mouse."

Damian took another step toward the kitchen. "I'm going to prepare a meal now. Feel free to watch me if you'd like. Either prepare your own food or abstain from ingestion all together, but remember this: we'll all have to eat sometime. Or else it matters not if the killer gets us in the end...for we'll have already starved. Now then, who will come with me? Mr. Proctor?"

The hunter shook his head.

"Mr. Schultz?"

Another head shake.

"Ms. Dobrzynski? Mr. Miller?"

"Sorry," Yusuf said. "Not hungry."

"Same," Rowan agreed, though Damian could tell she was lying. What else might she be lying about? he wondered. He had to say he didn't much like the look of her. What kind of young girl wore so much black anyway? One with black intentions, perhaps? They'd decided the gloves she wore were not incriminating, though Damian's suspicions had remained.

Yes, on Dr. Damian Donegan's list of possible suspects, the black-clad girl with the nervous eyes was certainly number one.

"I'll go," Nora said, and she clutched at her own stomach. "I'm too hungry not to." She stepped forward and smiled at him. It seemed like a genuine smile, though Damian suddenly found himself questioning her too.

Was hunger her sole motivation? Or was she only looking to keep an eye on him, make sure he didn't do anything to the food? Was she perhaps planning to contaminate it herself? It had not occurred to him before, but he realized now that a veterinarian would have access to a number of euthanizing drugs. Had he been wrong before about the killer's *modus operandi*? Were they not above—or below—murder by poison? More, were they the pretty, smiling woman standing before him?

All of these thoughts flashed through his head in a second. In the time it took for him to smile back.

"Very good," he said, and then turned back to the rest of the group. "We'll be off to the kitchen, then. Should anyone need us, we'll be but a shout away."

***

But a shout away.

The phrase echoed in Nora's mind. The wording was harmless enough, and the professor had said it amicably, though Nora had caught the silent message.

Keep an ear out.

Nora would certainly be doing that. She'd be keeping an eye out too. Maybe it was just because he was a larger man, but she found the professor's insistence upon eating suspicious. She found a great many things about him suspicious, if she was being honest. How he always sought to dominate the conversation, how he jumped from one conclusion to the next, and always absolutely, leaving zero room for nuance. Though he looked the part, Nora didn't think the man was even smart enough to be the distinguished college professor he claimed to be. Maybe it was just his age catching up with him, but he didn't exactly seem sound of mind. Just how *unsound* was he then, was the question that remained.

She meant to keep an eye on him, that was for sure. On Nora's list of possible suspects, the boisterous professor was by far number one.

But a shout away, she thought again.

And just who would be doing the shouting? And why?

***

It was maybe fifteen minutes after Damian and Nora left that Julian did the same. He couldn't take it anymore.

Rising from the chair he'd been sitting in, he was immediately met with looks from Yusuf, Rowan, and Proctor.

"Gonna go to the game room," he said, cocking a thumb to the side. Across the atrium, half of the space could be seen from the parlor.

No one objected, and Julian was soon on his way, though he felt eyes on his back. He'd tried to play it off like he was just bored, and at least part of that was true. Call him no better than the snots he babysat at Willy Wolfgang's, but he'd have much rather killed the time playing games than doing nothing. He figured anyone would.

But then, that was really only part of it.

The real reason he'd left was to get away from Proctor.

There was something about the rugged hunter Julian just didn't like, didn't trust. Something that sent the hairs prickling on the back of his neck, and made his stomach churn worse than it already was. It would have been one thing if the man was cordial, if he offset those cold looks with a smile or a nod every once in a while, but he didn't. He just stared at you. Made you think he knew something about you, something he didn't like, and hell if he'd ever tell you what it was.

Julian may not have been the most affable guy himself, but then, at least he tried to keep his head down. Tried to keep the chip on his shoulder from splintering off into everyone he met. Not this guy, though. Not Proctor. On Julian's list of possible suspects, the grim cowboy definitely ranked number one.

It was the pacing that had finally sent him over the edge. The hunter had been making rounds of the parlor, knocking on the walls, tapping on the floorboards, walking around like he was looking for something. Like there was something *hidden*.

Julian would leave him to it. In the meantime, he'd be in the game room.

He went to the pool table first, was just grabbing a cue when something caught his eye out the window, something that made him freeze.

He couldn't believe what he was seeing at first—didn't, even—though as he looked closer, it soon became undeniable. There was something on the fence. It sat atop the silver barrier like a bird on a telephone line, though a bird it certainly was not. While its color was black enough to pass as a crow or raven, the size and shape were all wrong. It was too big. Too...*mammalian*.

It was a bat.

It sat perfectly still upon the top of the fence, tucked far enough within the overhanging shade of the treeline that Julian was surprised he'd spotted it at all. Though he'd spotted it all right.

He never knew they could perch upright like that, bats. Had always figured they only ever hung upside down. The fence was far-off from the window, but even still, Julian could see the bat clearly, and it him. Maybe it was just his paranoia, but the creature seemed to be looking at him.

Judging him.

***

It was maybe ten minutes after Julian left that Proctor followed suit.

"Going to take a look around," he said, though he was halted by Yusuf's glare.

Rowan watched as the quarterback's eyes jumped nervously from the hunter in the doorway to Julian in the game room. The younger man could still be seen from the parlor. He stood at the window, looking at something outside.

Proctor followed Yusuf's gaze and laughed. "Don't worry, I ain't gonna hurt the kid." He jabbed a finger upward. "I'm going upstairs."

"For what?" Yusuf asked.

"Like I said, to take a look around." Proctor disappeared around the corner, and when Yusuf tensed like to get up and go after him, Rowan put a hand on his shoulder.

"It's okay," she said. "Let him go."

Yusuf caught her eye, and after a moment relaxed. He leaned back against the wall they were sitting against and shook his head.

"I don't trust that guy one bit," he said, jabbing a finger at the spot where Proctor had just stood. "If I had to make a list of possible suspects, *he'd* be number one."

Rowan disagreed. After Yusuf and Nora, the rugged hunter was probably who she trusted most. She said as much to Yusuf, though he continued to frown.

"I still don't like it," he said, shaking his head at the space where Proctor had stood. "What's he got to look around for anyway?"

Rowan shrugged. "More clues? The killer?"

"And if the killer's in the kitchen?" Yusuf asked, nodding in the direction Nora and Damian had gone. Rowan thought she could hear the faint sound of running water coming from down the hall. "Or in the game room?" he said quieter, nodding across the way. Julian had left the window now, was bent over the pool table.

"What, you think it's one of them?" Rowan asked. She meant all of them, though her eyes lingered on Julian. Despite him having stood up for her earlier, there was still something about the quiet kid that gave her pause. If she had to make a list of possible suspects, the boy in the purple Willy Wolfgang's shirt would probably be her number one.

"One of them," Yusuf shrugged, "or all of them." He leaned in close. "We can't ignore the possibility that one or more of them might be working together."

This turned Rowan's blood cold. The idea of one killer was bad enough, but two? Or even more than that? Up until this point, she'd lulled herself into a false sense of security. Safety in numbers, or whatever. It occurred to her then that she might not even have that to rely on, and the idea shook her. Yusuf must have seen the fear on her face, for he put a hand on her shoulder.

"Listen, it's just a theory. A scary one, but one we need to consider nonetheless."

Rowan took a breath to steady herself and nodded.

"The truth is," Yusuf began, pausing to look around before continuing, and he dropped his voice to a whisper. "I don't trust anybody in this house but *you*."

Rowan was touched, but she shook her head all the same.

"How can you?" she asked, swallowing hard. "How can you know for sure that I'm not in on it too?"

Yusuf considered this for a moment, then shrugged. "Just a feeling, I guess. We were on the train to the airport together, weren't we? And then on the plane too?" He gave another shrug. "That's gotta be something, right?" He shook his head. "I just trust you." He held out his hand. "Do you trust me?"

"I do," she said, taking it.

They met each other's eyes, and Rowan felt butterflies. For a moment, they remained there, but then something changed. Something in Yusuf's eyes. He turned his head down and pulled his hand away.

"Rowan...there's something I need to tell you," he said, and he was looking down now, at the burn on his palm.

"Yes?"

He met her gaze again, then quickly turned away. "Nevermind," he said, shaking his head. "I think it should wait. I'm...I'm feeling tired."

"Oh, okay. Is everything—?"

"Would you mind keeping watch while I get a little shut-eye?" he asked. "Sorry, it's just, I didn't get a lot of sleep last night and well..." His eyes slid nervously around the empty doorways. "...I wouldn't trust anyone else to do it."

"Of course," Rowan said immediately, though a part of her wished he'd stay awake. She liked talking to him. Liked *being* with him. That said, even she had to admit that he did look tired. Drained, almost.

"Thank you," he said, and began to position himself on the ground. "Maybe twenty or thirty minutes is all I'll need. Quick little power nap and then we can switch, you sleep and I watch, if you'd like."

"Sure," Rowan said with a smile. She hadn't gotten much sleep the previous night either. Too many thoughts in her head. Too many nightmares. "Have good dreams."

"Thanks," he said, and rolled over.

Rowan found it curious that Yusuf had foregone napping in one of the recliner chairs for the spot on the floor right beside her. Curious, though not at all upsetting.

She didn't think two whole minutes had passed before Yusuf was out, his breathing deep, the rise and fall of his chest a steady rhythm. Rowan found herself comforted by the quiet sound of it, and by the quarterback's very presence, too.

The memory of their hands clasped together kept replaying in her head, and the memory of what he'd said just now as well.

He trusted her. Out of everyone in the house, *he* trusted *her*.

She decided she trusted him too. She felt safe around him. And so much so that it wasn't long before she began to drift off herself, lulled by the quiet sounds of his slumber, and slowly carried into a sleep of her own.

***

Proctor was just coming downstairs again when he heard the scream.

High-pitched and close by, he thought he knew who it came from, and where...and probably why, too.

He came into the parlor at the same time as Julian, Damian, and Nora, the first with a pool cue in hand, the others with an apron and oven mitts respectively. Only Yusuf and Rowan had remained in the parlor, though they were far from how Proctor had left them.

"What?" Damian shouted as he emerged from the hallway. "What is it?"

He asked these questions, though the panic in his voice said he already knew. And how couldn't he? They'd all heard the scream, and there was no mistaking what it meant.

Yusuf Miller lay dead on the floor, a grisly slash through his throat. Beside him, sobbing and shaking, sat Rowan, a kitchen knife in one gloved hand, the small girl up to her elbows in blood.

Chapter Eight

The Room

"It wasn't me. I-I know what it looks like...and I know it's bad. B-b-but, it wasn't *me*."

Rowan was still sobbing. Hyperventilating, really. She just kept looking back at Yusuf. Much like everyone was, though not Nora. She couldn't stop looking at Rowan. The young girl's sleeves used to be pitch-black like the rest of her outfit. Only, now they were a brownish color, completely drenched in the red of Yusuf's blood.

Rowan's eyes, darting frantically around the room, finally found Nora's, and she rose as they did. "Nora—" she began, and moved to take a step forward, though Damian stopped her.

"You stay right where you are!" he bellowed, and Rowan froze. Proctor too, Nora realized, had stepped forward, one hand shoved deep in a jacket pocket.

"Drop the knife," he said, nodding to the blade still clenched in the girl's hand.

Rowan's eyes fell to the knife and then widened, as if she were surprised to see it there. She dropped it, horrified, and took a step back from where it clattered on the ground.

"It seems the mystery of the missing knife has been solved," Damian said, and his eyes narrowed on Rowan. "Ms. Dobrzynski had been hiding it all along!"

"No!" Rowan cried, and she shook her head frantically. "No, no, no, no, no! It's not...it's not what it looks like. I didn't have it, I..." She turned back to Yusuf for a moment and then squeezed her eyes shut. "*I pulled it out!*"

Another fit of sobs followed this, so raw and guttural that Nora's heart could not help but ache for the girl, though she stayed moving to comfort her. The black-clad artist was covered in entirely too much blood for that.

"Oh, a likely story," Damian laughed. "And what, a ghost stuck it in?"

"The killer did!" Rowan cried. "Or—" Her eyes suddenly went wide, and she took a step back. "One of *you*."

"Oh, that's logical," Damian said, shaking his head. "Here stands a woman with a knife in her hand, blood-soaked to the hip, and yet one of *us* is responsible?" He raised his eyebrows at the rest of the group. "Tell me, do any of you believe it?"

No one said they did, though Nora noticed that no one said they *didn't*, either.

She found herself running through the past thirty minutes. Had she noticed anything strange? She'd been in the kitchen with Damian all the while, keeping an eye on him, though there'd been a brief period in which she hadn't. A short trip to the restroom had put the professor well beyond her eyesight. Two minutes was all it had been. Two minutes, and she'd found him exactly where she'd left him. She thought the odds of him leaving during that time slim, though not impossible. Could the professor have killed Yusuf in that window?

And what of Proctor and Julian? What had the two of them been doing?

All signs currently pointed to Rowan, but could they be trusted?

“I don’t know what to believe,” Proctor said finally. “But I do know we’d be stupid to let her keep walking around like she is.” He stepped forward, one hand still shoved deep in that jacket pocket, and Nora’s eyes went wide.

“What exactly are you suggesting?” she demanded, stepping forward too, between Rowan and Proctor, and against her better judgment. Her eyes stayed glued to the hunter’s pocket. They’d done a pat down search for weapons already, but if they’d missed something...

Proctor must have noticed her looking, for he removed his hand to reveal what lay within: a pair of handcuffs.

“I’m suggesting we cuff her,” he said. “Put her some place where she can’t hurt anyone.” The hunter’s gaze turned to Rowan. “Some place where we can keep an eye on her.”

“An excellent idea, Mr. Proctor!” Damian said, stepping forward. “Might I suggest one of the upstairs bedrooms? The doors have locks, and I believe one of those headboards would make for the perfect anchor.”

Proctor nodded like in agreement and took another step forward, opening the cuffs as he did.

Rowan’s eyes went wide.

“No...no, no, no, please,” she stammered. “Don’t do this. Y-you can’t do this! I’m innocent! I’m—”

"Covered in a dead man's blood," Damian said, and so forcefully that Rowan began to sob again.

"No, you don't understand," she said, looking down at her hands. It was as if she'd thrust them into a bucket of paint. "This...this wasn't me. I was just trying to help him...to *save* him!"

"And if that is true, rest assured you will be vindicated. Though until then, I'm afraid all signs point to you." The professor stepped forward, spoke next in a gentler voice. "Look at it from our perspective, Ms. Dobrzynski. To us, it clearly appears that *you* are the killer."

Rowan just shook her head.

"Not all of you," she said softly, and she met the group with hard, bloodshot eyes. "Not the one who actually did it."

"By all means, tell us then," Damian said, the boom in his voice back in an instant. "If you're so sure it was one of us, that is." He gestured to the rest of the group. "Tell us who."

Rowan seemed to search the room with her eyes, jumping between the different figures, desperately trying, with an ever-furrowing brow, to decide. She ultimately scrunched them shut, turned to the ground and shook her head.

"I...I don't know," she said, and though her head was down, Nora could see new tears dropping off her cheeks.

"Then I'm sorry, Ms. Dobrzynski, but I'm afraid this is how it must be." Damian turned to the rest of them. "The decision is unanimous, is it not?"

Proctor, cuffs still in hand, obviously agreed, and when Damian turned to Julian, the boy nodded too, though he looked solemn.

It was left to Nora, and as all eyes fell upon her, so did the accused.

"Nora, please," Rowan stammered, her breath beginning to hitch all over again. "You can't let them do this. You *can't*!"

Nora could hardly hold her gaze. The girl's eyes, hopeless as they were, certainly didn't seem like those of a killer, but then, those blood-soaked hands certainly did. Though some small part of her felt wrong doing so, she finally shook her head.

"I'm sorry, Rowan, but this is how it has to be. If you're innocent...or if you're not, I hope you understand why."

Nora nodded to Proctor, and the hunter took another step forward.

Rowan immediately took one back, flinching as she hit the wall behind her. Eyes wide with terror, her voice came out as little more than a whisper.

"Please...don't leave me alone."

"We won't," Nora promised. "We'll put you in a central location, somewhere close by so we can all keep an eye on you. For our safety, *and* for yours."

She nodded around the room to make clear this was a condition. No one objected.

"A fine idea, Ms. Inwood," Damian said with a nod. "Now, Ms. Dobrzynski, will you come willingly?"

Reluctantly, Rowan raised her blood-soaked wrists, and Proctor cuffed them. As the hunter led her away, Nora met her eye and gave her a nod.

It'll be okay, she tried to say through it.

And she hoped it was true.

***

It was sunset when Julian's turn came to stand guard by Rowan's door. By her temporary prison.

They had decided to lock her in one of the downstairs bathrooms, that way she could relieve herself as needed and begin to wash off the blood, too. The water wasn't running anymore, so Julian thought she must have finished, though that metallic scent still hung heavy in the air.

Julian swore he could smell it everywhere he went.

He approached the door slowly, nervously, adjusting his posture as if she might be able to see him through it, though he knew that was impossible. He ultimately decided to turn around, rest his back against the door's front.

"Hey, Rowan," he tried after a minute. "How are you doing?"

No response.

For a moment, he feared the worst. He feared that he might open the door to find the pale girl in black slaughtered too, though he quickly thought better. She was probably just being quiet, probably felt like she had nothing to say. Julian knew a thing or two about that.

He tried a different approach.

"I'm sorry about Yusuf. He...he seemed like a nice guy."

For a long moment, there was only more silence, but then, weakly:

"Yeah."

She was still alive, then. That was good. He nodded and continued.

"I didn't get to know him for that long, but I liked him," Julian said, and it was the truth.

"Yeah," Rowan said. "I liked him too."

Another long moment passed in silence, and then she spoke again.

"Hey, Julian?"

"Yes?"

"Do you think we're all going to die here?"

Julian swallowed hard. He didn't know what to say.

"No," he finally managed. "I...I hope not."

He might have said more, but was stopped by a sharp pain in his stomach. It was a gnawing pain, and it kept getting worse.

"Hey, kid," came a voice from ahead of him. Proctor had emerged from the next room.

"Yeah?"

"It's getting dark. We're going out to fire the second flare." He nodded toward the bathroom. "She still in there?"

Julian nodded.

"Door locked?"

When Julian hesitated to test the handle, Proctor did it himself. It was.

The hunter stepped back and fixed Julian with a long stare. Eventually, he nodded.

"Come on, then," he said, turning away.

"But—" Julian began, though stopped as the hunter looked back.

"But what?"

Julian shot a sideward glance to the bathroom door before dropping his voice low. "Didn't we say we weren't going to leave her?" He shook his head nervously. "Shouldn't one of us stay?"

"So that whoever does can kill the girl while the rest are away?"

"What?" Julian said, taken aback. "No—"

"Or maybe you think two people should stay back," the hunter continued, voice dry and apathetic as ever. "Only, that don't work either." He held up two fingers on either hand, drew them apart. "Leaves both parties susceptible...assuming the killer still walks free."

Proctor shot Julian a long, dangerous look at this, the likes of which made the boy's skin crawl.

"No matter how you spin it, keeping together's the smartest bet. Lets us keep an eye on one another...if not on the one detained."

His eyes slid to the bathroom door before falling to the ground.

"Check the handle again if you must, but then come on. She'll be fine for as long as we're gone. Hell, behind a locked door with the key inside? She's probably the safest of us all."

He stalked back into the other room and Julian reluctantly made to follow, though Rowan's voice made him freeze.

"I think we are," she said quietly, and Julian swallowed hard, finally turning to face the door which separated them with wide eyes.

"What?"

"I think we are," Rowan said again. "I think we're all going to die."

***

"We shouldn't have left her alone," Nora said, halting suddenly to look back at the house. "We said we wouldn't leave her alone."

They were outside the manor now, making their slow way to the outbuilding. And it was a slow way. Mostly on account of Nora's hesitation.

"For the last time, Ms. Inwood, we're not," Damian snapped, having grown tired of the delays. "The manor is in our sight, is it not? And all of us within its cursed fence?"

The veterinarian cut him a nasty look.

"You know what I mean," she said, and shook her head at the house again. "One or two of us should have stayed back. We don't need all four of us to shoot a flare off."

"Oh, but I'm afraid we do," Damian said. "Do you recall what happens, Ms. Inwood, when one or two of us become isolated in this place? Death! Death is what happens every single time! The killer sees their opportunity, and seizes it!"

"So then why are we leaving Rowan by herself?" Nora cried, rising to match the professor's volume. She threw a hand back at the manor. "Who's to say the killer won't seize *that* opportunity?"

"Nothing! Though I'd say there is ample evidence to suggest that Ms. Dobrzynski and the killer are one in the same."

"And if they're not?"

"Then I suggest we four keep a keen eye on one another," he said, gaze shifting slowly around the group. "Pardon my bluntness, but I would assume I'm not alone in suspecting the lot of you as well."

The silence that followed said he wasn't, and the way it drew out was enough to make Damian's skin crawl. He shivered harshly.

"Pray, let us be hasty about it too. The longer we argue, the longer Ms. Dobrzynski remains vulnerable, and we as well." He let his eyes sweep warily about their surroundings. It was full dark now, so dim that not even the silhouette of the fence could be seen, though Damian knew it was there. He could *feel* it. He shivered again. "I say, a darkness like this, paired with our circumstances...it is enough to drive one mad."

"Come on, then," Proctor urged, and they did.

By the time they arrived at the outbuilding, Damian could no longer see his own body beneath him. Struggling to define his immediate vicinity, he bumped into Julian for what felt like the third or fourth time.

"Damned shadows!" he growled, thrashing his arms through the air as if doing so might tear them away. "Why didn't we take the blasted thing inside with us? Do we even know where it is?"

"Where'd you leave it, kid?" Proctor asked.

"Here," Julian said. He must have handed the thing to Proctor, for Damian soon heard the hunter's steady footfalls.

"Come on," he said, and seemed to exit the outbuilding.

Following at a slower pace, Damian said: "You're quite adept at moving in the dark, Mr. Proctor. A trick of the trade?"

"Something like that."

"Well don't go too fast," Nora called, even further behind than Damian. "The last thing we need is to get separated."

"Don't worry," Proctor called back. "We're almost there."

Damian walked maybe fifteen paces more, and all of them totally blind, before being stopped suddenly by a hand at his shoulder.

"That's far enough, doc," Proctor said, and for a moment, Damian was stupefied.

The professor could not even see his own hand in front of his face, let alone place it on the shoulder of another. Proctor's touch had been gentle, though it sent Damian's hairs standing nonetheless. Had Proctor merely heard his footfalls, or could the hunter *see in the dark*?

"Right," he said, shrugging off the rugged man's hand. "Let's get this over with, then. I fear this darkness has grown tiring."

If there were any nods of agreement, Damian couldn't see them.

He felt a chill run down his spine. Despite the blackness, he could not shake the feeling that he was being watched.

Proctor seemed to step forward then, and in a low voice whispered: "*Que sea lo que Dios quiera.*"

There was a sharp hiss as he shot the flare off, followed immediately by a high-pitched whine as the flickering beacon soared high into the sky. It certainly seemed brighter than the one they'd shot off that afternoon; its fiery light cut through the blackness and bathed the backyard in a dark red glow.

In the moment of illumination, Damian saw all of the group members' faces, the three of them pitched in warped, shadowy grimaces before the empty yard. But then, had that been all he'd seen?

Had there been something else farther off? Something by the fence line, large and crouched and enshrouded in black? No, he decided as the darkness returned. It had been but a shift in the shadows. A trick of the mind. His own fearful thoughts manifest.

But then he heard a footstep.

It was a faraway thing, and delicate too. Thoughtful. The kind of footstep something takes when it wishes not to be heard, though it had been. Damian could not deny it.

"Did you hear that?" he hissed, and his voice came out shriller than usual. Tinged with fear.

"What?" Nora hissed back, though he thought he heard her move, shift around to look behind her. Proctor and Julian said nothing.

"By the fence line..." Damian said, trailing off. The silence was immense now. Unnatural. Despite their being in the middle of the woods, not a single insect was singing. They might have remained forever in that quiet, wide-eyed and wary in that eternal stillness, but then it came again.

Another footstep, as far-off and delicate as the last, but this time irrefutable.

"There's something over there," Damian whispered, barely a breath on his lips, though the silence assured that he was heard.

As if in response, a third footstep fell, and Damian could stand it no longer.

"Stay back, you!" he cried, struggling to find the gusto in his voice. "Whoever you are, stay back or—"

The footsteps took off running then, and any more words died in Damian's throat.

"Run!" he cried. "*Run!*"

And they all did. Or at least, he thought they all did. In the pitch-blackness, it was impossible to tell. Damian heard a collection of breaths and a smattering of footsteps, though there was no telling what was what, nor who was who.

At least for the moment, he didn't care.

In the chaotic dark, it was every man and woman for themselves.

***

Eventually, the four of them found their way back to the manor. Proctor first, followed by Damian and Julian, and Nora last. According to Damian's watch, it had been twenty minutes since they'd initially left the house, and maybe five since they'd shot the flare, though that last bit had felt more like an eternity. He sat in the atrium now, catching his breath with the others. By the looks on their faces, they all looked as terrified as he felt. Even Proctor looked spooked. Though they were all safely inside, the hunter stayed close to the door, his eyes never leaving the front windows.

"Mr. Proctor," Damian said finally, still breathing hard. "Have you any idea what just pursued us?"

The hunter shook his head, though the grimace on his face said different.

"Did you get a look at it, Damian?" Nora asked. "Could it have just been an animal?"

"Not a very good look, no," he admitted, shaking his head. "I suppose it *could* have been a creature," he offered, though he bore a doubtful grimace of his own.

"At least we all made it," Julian said, and Nora's eyes suddenly went wide.

"Rowan," she breathed, and took off for the bathroom.

"Ms. Inwood!" Damian cried, though the veterinarian was already around the corner. "Ms. Inwood, hold on!"

The party followed suit, nearly sprinting through the manor until they arrived at Rowan's holding cell, though a cell it was no longer. The door was wide open, and within, a familiar scene had been laid out.

"No!" Nora cried, bringing her hands to her face.

Julian turned away. Proctor and Damian only stared.

Rowan Dobrzynski lay in the bathtub, her throat slashed open the same as the rest, though that was not what caught Damian's eye.

A word had been written on the wall beside her, seven jagged letters scrawled in blood. It was the artist's final work, and it stared back at her four survivors with malicious contempt.

Traitor, it read.

Chapter Nine

The Message

"Ms. Inwood..." Damian began, placing a hand on Nora's shoulder, though she immediately cringed away.

"Don't you touch me!" she spat, spinning around on the professor. She then took a step back, shooting glares at Julian and Proctor too. "Don't any of you touch me!"

"Ms. Inwood, please," Damian said, raising his hands in a placating gesture. "I was merely trying to comfort—"

"Don't!" she cried. "You really think I want *comfort* from any one of you right now?" She shook her head. "No, I suspected it before, but now there's no denying it." She looked from the bloody letters on the wall to the professor. "*You* can't be trusted."

"*Me?*" he cried, offended.

"Any of you!" she said, raising her hands above her head. "Rowan made it pretty clear, didn't she? One of us is a traitor!"

"Oh, come now, Ms. Inwood. Surely, you can't take *that* as conclusive evidence." He gestured to the painted word and shook his head. "For all we know, the killer could have written it themselves!"

"I don't think so," Proctor said. The hunter had crossed to the tub, was closely examining the blood on the wall, and the body below it.

"And why exactly is that, Mr. Proctor?"

"'Traitor,'" he said, shaking his head at the word. "It's too general."

Damian laughed, a cruel, haughty thing. "You were hoping maybe for *quisling*?"

Proctor shot him a look and the professor's smile vanished.

"Can you explain what you mean?" Nora asked, looking to Proctor.

The hunter shrugged. "Why write traitor?" he said, looking from Nora to the wall again. "Why not just write who?"

"Because then it might seem even more suspicious," Julian said, stepping forward, and Nora nearly jumped. The boy had a way of blending in, she'd noticed. A way of fading to the background. She made a mental note to keep a closer eye on him.

"If the killer was trying to frame someone," he continued, "chances are they'd be more specific. The fact that this isn't makes it seem more legit. Or, at least...that's what I think."

The boy took a step back after finishing, clutching his stomach as if speaking in front of them all had physically pained him. Absently, Nora wondered if it had.

"I agree," she said, nodding slowly, and Proctor did too. Damian was the only one still unconvinced.

"Well I'm sorry but I don't," he said, crossing his arms tightly. "If you're all so sure that Ms. Dobrzynski's murder was committed by one of us, then who? And better yet, how? She was not left alone for very long, firstly. And for the short period in which she *was,* the four of us were all together! Were we not?"

"I couldn't see you," Nora said, shaking her head. "I couldn't see any of you."

"Wha—? You mean in the dark?" Damian sputtered. "Well, I hardly think that should matter...we heard each other's voices, didn't we? And the flare! Yes, we saw each other in the glow of the—"

"But then there was a commotion." Nora interjected. "Everyone was running. There was a period where someone could have slipped away." She looked down at Rowan. "A period where they could have *killed.*"

"I say, an incredibly short period!" Damian exclaimed, still disbelieving. "Why, for someone to do as you suggest...they'd need to be *terribly* quick."

"It's been a day and they've killed five already," Julian said. "I don't think their quickness is really in question."

Nora nodded in agreement. "Whoever's doing this, they're good."

"They're a monster," Proctor said, eyeing the room.

"So find them, then," Damian said, taking a step toward the hunter. "Or was that fairy-tale title of yours just for show?"

"Watch it, doc," Proctor said, matching the professor's step with one of his own. He cut a deep, serious frown. "Wouldn't want things to get ugly, now."

"Oh, I'm afraid they're *far* past ugly."

The men were but inches apart now, staring each other down like a pair of feral dogs. The mastiff versus the Doberman.

Nora felt something like a chihuahua coming in between them, but she did so anyway.

"You two cut it out," she said, pushing herself into the middle and forcing each man back a step. She slid a glare between them. "That's the last thing we need right now."

It took a moment, but both men eventually backed off, though their hackles stayed up. Nora supposed there was no changing that; hers were up too.

"It's been a long day," she said, speaking diplomatically. "We're all running on little sleep and even less food. I suggest we all go to the pantry, grab something we're sure is *sealed*, and retire to different rooms for the night."

"You really think splitting up again is a good idea?" Julian asked, looking around nervously.

"Honestly, I'm not sure anymore. We've already seen what happens when we sleep in shifts. If everyone locks their doors and windows, I think the bedrooms might just be our safest bet. Besides, I think it would do everyone some good to get away from each other for a little while."

"Agreed," Damian said, still glaring at Proctor.

The hunter just sneered.

"Okay then it's decided. We'll lock ourselves in for the night. But we have to deal with this first." Her eyes fell to Rowan's body, still slumped and bloodied in the bathtub. "We can't leave her like this."

And so they took care of it, took Rowan's body down to the basement and covered it with a sheet like the rest. There were five of them down there now, the makings of a mausoleum. Nora tried her best to ignore them, tried to ignore the way their blood stained those white sheets red. Though even after turning away, she found the image remained in her mind.

Once they had all chosen their food items and returned to their rooms—Nora with but a box of cereal—she found herself thinking again about Rowan, and about her message. She found herself wondering if maybe it had been incomplete, if maybe, in her last moments, the dying girl had not had the energy for a final letter, an *S*. Of course, that would have turned *traitor* to *traitors*, but then, wasn't that also true? More than just the killer, in the end...hadn't they all betrayed her?

Though she'd triple-checked the locks, moved the dresser in front of the window, and both nightstands in front of the door, Nora doubted if she'd get any rest that night. Even if she did manage to fall asleep, she knew it would be a sleep filled with nightmares.

***

Proctor lay awake in his bed, hat on his chest, the remnants of a barely picked at trail mix on the nightstand beside him. He found himself thinking about the day's events, running through the details. Was there anything he'd missed? And of that he hadn't, what could it mean?

He found himself thinking about the bathroom, the one where the quiet girl had gotten her throat slit in the tub.

There'd been no mirror in that bathroom. No mirrors in the entire house, so far as he'd seen, and he'd been looking. He wondered if anyone else had noticed.

***

Julian kept his eyes glued to the door as he gnawed through his third bag of potato chips. He found the bottom of it and cursed himself for not grabbing a fourth. He hadn't realized how hungry he'd been. The little sustenance had helped his stomach some, though the pain still lingered.

Something told him it would remain all night.

***

Damian had no intention of sleeping that night, though the instant he finished his porridge and his head hit the pillow, the old professor was out like a light. It had been a long, busy day.

Chapter Ten

The Wait

The next morning, the party members awoke to find that they had all survived the night.

"Good to see that there are as many of us today as there were last evening," Damian said when they had all gathered in the dining hall. "I trust everyone slept well?"

"Like a baby," Nora joked, though she did not smile. To Julian, it didn't look like the woman had slept a wink.

"I am glad to hear it, Ms. Inwood," the professor said, rubbing his own tired eyes. "I'm afraid my own sleep was much plagued by nightmares." He turned to Julian and Proctor. "Mr. Schultz, Mr. Proctor, might the two of you have fared any better?"

Julian shook his head.

Proctor didn't respond.

"I suppose it is to be expected," Damian said with a nod. "Anyone who could sleep soundly after bearing witness to what we have, why...I suppose they'd have to be quite *cold*."

If the professor's eyes lingered on the hunter after saying this, they left before the rugged man could respond.

"Time for breakfast, then?" Damian said, turning toward the pantry. "After the nights we've had, I should hope Ms. Wilmore was in possession of some *coffee*."

As it turned out, she was. Cases of the stuff, actually, and all of them of the sealed, pre-bottled variety that assured they could all drink with peace of mind. Or at least, peace of mind at a distance of at least six feet, and with due care that the only things which passed the rims of their cups were their own lips.

"I'm afraid our diets may have to consist solely of processed food for the near future," Damian said, opening a small pack of cookies that would serve as his breakfast. "To think, an entire mansion around us, chock-full of foodstuffs with an industrial kitchen to boot...and we are resigned to gas station cuisine at best." He shook his head. "When you stop to think about it, I suppose it really is quite *mad*."

The professor laughed then, though no one joined him. It was a joyless, somewhat unhinged sound, and Julian found himself wondering if the old man was on the brink of madness himself.

They ate anyway. Breakfast first, and then lunch, when the time came. Always sealed food items, and always while watching each other in long, stern bouts of silence.

When conversation did break out, it was short, terse, and always with a forced quality—an air of suspicion running all the way through it. Julian found it horribly unpleasant, though he found the silence worse. Anytime he'd find himself staring at one of his three housemates for too long, he'd turn to find another one of them staring at him, only for them all to turn, subtly switch partners, and start the whole process over again.

Some relief came when they decided to move to the game room. There they could dispel some of their nervous energy, could direct their mental focuses onto something other than each other, though tensions certainly remained. Every move felt like a challenge, every decision a clue to consider.

Why exactly did Nora go to that side of the foosball table? Might Damian decide to stab Proctor with the pool cue in his hand? Might he decide to stab me?

Thoughts and questions like these whipped around Julian's head like balloons in a tornado. Many were absurd, he knew, though still he could not help but think them. And by the looks on the others' faces, by their mannerisms and silent words, he thought it likely that they were thinking them too.

More than a few times, the group strayed to the front porch, huddling on that front stoop like a band of Christmas carolers, though they did not sing. They hardly even talked. Their eyes stayed locked on that front gate, and on the forest beyond. On that road where Julian kept wishing he'd see a car drive up, deposit some forest ranger or good samaritan before them and act as their salvation, though it never happened. The road remained empty, and they remained trapped.

Trapped in the manor, and trapped with each other.

Julian still felt that Proctor was the worst. He could never tell what the man was thinking, and he certainly couldn't trust him. But then, the more he stewed on it, and the longer the dreadful day dragged on, the more he realized he couldn't trust any of them.

And all along his stomach hurt. Aching with the old pain of yesterday, and throbbing with the new pain of today. The pain of anticipation. The pain of fear.

It was only when evening began to approach, when the sky turned orange and the shadows cast by the trees grew large and ominous that they abandoned their outdoor waiting.

Julian thought it was something about being out in the woods at night that had a way of unnerving people, that made them turn in early and lock their doors behind them. The group certainly seemed unnerved, but then, it had been an unnerving weekend. Maybe it was just that they dreaded spending another night in the manor where they'd seen so many murdered. Julian certainly felt as much. But then, maybe, he thought, it was something else too.

"Good God," Damian said suddenly, startling Julian where he stood beside him. "One would think the firing of two flares might have attracted some attention by now."

"Got somewhere to be?" Proctor asked, eyeing the professor carefully.

"As a matter of fact, I do. In my study with a book in hand. Or perhaps in a mental ward, given what this weekend has forced me to endure."

There were some nods of agreement at that, and Nora perked her head up.

"Maybe we could move to the study upstairs," she suggested, and her eyes fell. "Where we...where we found Elijah." She paused for a moment before continuing. "There were a lot of books up there. Perhaps we could pass the time better."

Though the proposal was perfectly ordinary, and her words even optimistic, Julian thought the veterinarian looked more anxious than ever.

Nevertheless, they decided her idea was a good one, and soon the lot of them were in the study, standing at all four corners of the book-laden room, their eyes shifting constantly between the countless pages and each other.

The book Elijah had been reading was still on the ground, along with a dark red stain. Julian was just moving to pick it up when the lights flickered, and he froze as they went out for good.

The room went black. There was movement in the shadows. A gasp. And then the lights returned.

When Julian could see again, he registered that the room was much the same as he'd seen it seconds earlier. Though there was at least one difference.

A bloodied knife sat on the carpet, closest to Julian, though in the cramped library, they were all in proximity. His eyes immediately dashed between the others, checking for differences. Checking for *death.*

They were all still standing, and so for a moment, it appeared as if nothing else had changed. But then Damian fell to his knees, a wound at his throat revealed, and it was clear that the killer had struck again.

No sooner had the professor collapsed upon the carpet, his blood spilling over the same spot Elijah's had, that Julian heard a distinct clicking sound behind him.

He didn't have to hear Nora's gasp to know what it was.

The hunter had pulled a weapon on him, on both of them, or so his oscillating aim ensured. It was a peculiar weapon, a kind of wooden crossbow. Strange enough to appear custom made, and small enough to be easily missed in a pat down search.

Julian knew they hadn't been thorough enough.

"Proctor," Nora said, taking a step back. "What are you—"

"Don't either of you make another move," he said, locking in a bolt with a final, threatening click. "Unless of course, you'd like to be on the receiving end."

Julian watched Nora's eyes flicker between him and the hunter. They were wide and terrified. Julian wanted to say something, but his throat felt woven shut.

Keeping very still, Nora spoke again slowly.

"Proctor, why do you have that thing? Why are you aiming it at *us*?"

"Told you I was a hunter, didn't I?" he said. "As for why I'm aiming it where I am, well, I think that part's obvious." He nodded to the knife on the ground, and then to Damian. "One of you just killed the doc."

"What?" Nora began, shaking her head rapidly, though when Proctor shifted his aim to her, she stopped. "You...you don't know that," she said. "You can't *prove*—"

"Who was it then?" Proctor said suddenly, and loudly enough to make Nora flinch. "Look around, *amiga*. No open doors. No broken windows. No way out."

The hunter paused to look around the room himself before shaking his head.

"You see, I wanted to believe it was somebody else. Some phantom killer we could never quite get a glimpse of. Some ghost. But *this*?" He gestured again to dead professor and shook his head. "This cinches it. The killer's been one of us all along. And they're right here in this room."

"You're the one holding the weapon," Julian said, finally finding the words in his throat.

"And that's how it's going to stay, *hermano*," Proctor said, eyes grim. "Unless one of you says who did it, I'll just kill you both."

"No," Nora said, "Y-you can't."

"I can," Proctor said with a nod. "But I don't have to. Not if one of you fesses up."

"This is wrong. You don't even—"

"I'm going to count to ten," he said, and began.

"Ten.

"Nine."

"No—"

"Eight.

"Seven.

"Stop..."

"Six."

"Please!"

"Five.

"Four."

"*Please...*"

"Three.

"Two."

"Wait!" Julian shouted, and pointed to the back wall. Proctor's sights had been on Nora, but the speed with which he rotated was enough to make Julian's heart skip a beat. He realized his hand was shaking.

Having followed his finger all the same, Proctor was now regarding the back wall with confusion. Though his eyes jumped between it and Julian, his aim never faltered. "What?"

"The shelf," Julian said, still frozen mid-point. It was all he could do to keep his arm somewhat steady.

"What about it?" the hunter growled, though he seemed to be looking more closely now. Had he noticed what Julian had?

"It...it looks indented. Like you could just pull it open or something. Like it's a *door.*"

For a long moment, Proctor just stared, hard at Julian and Nora both, then he barked:

"Window," and he motioned to the side of the room opposite the indented shelf. "Move."

They did, and the hunter was given room to inspect the wall in question. Julian was still surprised he'd noticed it, though the longer he looked, the more obvious it became. Where one shelf ended and the next began, there was an indentation. It protruded by only about an inch or two, but against the conformity of the rest of the room, the discrepancy was hard to unsee.

Proctor seemed to notice it too, though when he investigated, trying to push or pull it further, the thing wouldn't budge. He looked close to giving up when Nora spoke, her voice still tinged with fear, but firm.

"The books," she said, nodding to the colorful spines which lined the shelf in question. "Try the books."

Proctor shot the woman a suspicious look, though ultimately did as she said. One by one, he began to pull the books off the shelf. Most just spilled out, toppling to the floor like the one left by Elijah. Though when the hunter came to a particularly large book three shelves down, something different happened.

Rather than moving by itself, the tome moved with the three next to it, as if the four books had been glued together, and as if they were not books at all, but a lever.

They fell part way back from the shelf, staying attached at an angle, and as they moved away, so too did the entire shelf, swinging back on hidden hinges to reveal a previously concealed stairway beyond. A secret passage.

"No way out, huh?" Nora said, glaring at Proctor.

The hunter gave a slow nod, though he did not lower his crossbow.

"You," he said, pointing at Julian. "Go down first." He turned to Nora. "Then you."

Under threat of crossbow, Julian complied, nearing the stairway carefully. He came to its edge and felt his stomach lurch.

"Go," Proctor commanded, and so he did.

The passage was dark, and it led down. Julian had a feeling he knew where it went.

Chapter Eleven

The Basement

The stairs led to the basement. Because of course they did. The rest of this weekend had been the stuff of a horror novel, hadn't it? And so as Nora made her slow way down those steep, dark steps, ever aware of Proctor's crossbow at her back, she couldn't shake the feeling that this particular story was nearing its end.

They arrived to find the manor's underground much the way they'd left it. Empty but for that busted cage, those red and white sheets, and the dead people beneath them. Though they searched diligently, they found no third party, no killer hiding in the shadows. For the most part, the place was unchanged, though Nora could not help but notice that those four bodies had begun to smell.

"Nothing," Proctor said finally, shaking his head at the decrepit room. He looked up the main stairs. "And we locked that door, too." He paused a beat. "Though perhaps we should double-check..." He eyed Nora and Julian crossly. "Be back in a minute." He made a motion to them with the crossbow. "You two stay right there."

The hunter turned then, started up the main stairs and was quickly engulfed by their shadows. It was so dark down there, lit only by a single bulb and the dim glow of twilight, that Nora wondered if she might be able to do the same, retreat to an empty corner and conceal herself in the gloom. She needed to find some way out, after all. And she needed to do it fast.

As it stood, she had two escape routes: back up the hidden staircase, or through the shattered basement window. But then, where would she go from there? Where would she hide? Nowhere the hunter wouldn't find her, she was sure. And what of Julian? Would she abandon the young man? Should she try and devise a way to subdue Proctor with his help? Could the two of them even win that fight?

So loud were the thoughts in her head, that she didn't notice the quiet movement behind her, or the fact that the hunter's had been irregular. He re-emerged from the darkness of the stairs suddenly, and Nora was chilled by the realization that he'd never truly gone up them, had ascended only far enough to conceal himself, and then watched from the shadows.

He descended now with a grim look and his crossbow aimed right at her.

"Don't you take another step," he said, and it was all Nora could do not to take one back on instinct.

"Proctor," she breathed, slowly putting her hands up. "Please...I—"

"Not you," he said, and nodded to something behind her. "*Him.*"

It was only then that Nora registered the quiet movement she'd sensed behind her, and she turned to find Julian inches away, a blade in his hand, a crazed look in his eye.

"I'd take a step back if I were you," Proctor warned, and he nodded at Julian. "That boy there's a *killer*."

"Julian..." Nora said, disbelieving at first, though the farther she backed away, and the longer she looked at him, the more she *did* believe. Julian looked afraid, as afraid as Nora felt. It was the same fear she'd seen on his face all weekend. Only...it seemed different now. As if there'd been something she'd missed before. Something that had gone unrecognized, though had silently been there all along.

Something guilty.

"But...why?" she said finally.

"You haven't figured it out yet?" Proctor asked, directing the question at Nora. When she shook her head, he just grinned.

"It's a strange house we've spent the last few nights in, no? And I mean more than just the paint job. Take a look around," he said, gesturing up to the manor at large. "Think back. I'm sure you've noticed the signs. No mirrors, dark black curtains on every window...an entire mansion, and not a speck of wood in it." He met her eyes. "You know how hard it is to build a house like this without using wood, amiga?"

Nora shook her head.

"It's hard," Proctor said, and his gaze shifted to Julian. "It's *real* hard."

Nora still didn't understand. She shook her head again. "Okay so the house is strange...what's your point?"

"Oh, come on, doc," Proctor said. "*Think* about it. The bathrooms in this house have a lot of chrome and brushed nickel fashions, but no silver. That pantry's got just about every herb and spice you could ever need, but no garlic." The hunter shot Nora a knowing look at this, and her eyes went wide.

"You don't mean..."

Proctor nodded and turned to Julian.

"That boy right there is a *vampire*."

The young man did not reply, though his eyes were about as wide as Nora's. Wide and guilty.

"You see, I'd been suspecting a vampire for some time," Proctor explained. "I'd been suspecting one of our own, too—only the correlation never quite fit. One of us? A vampire? But we were all out there in the sun—and for long enough that any true vampire would have burned to a crisp." He shook his head. "Yeah, for a while there, it didn't work. Seemed *impossible*." He tapped a finger to his temple. "But then I started thinking.

"I started thinking about that long, thick hair of yours," he said, nodding to Julian. "Nice and dark. I started thinking about the way you always kept your hands in your pockets, shoved down nice and deep." Proctor grinned. "It's a neat trick, *niño*. Keeps the skin safe."

Nora found herself trying to remember a time when she'd seen Julian in the sun. A time when—even if it had only been for a moment—she'd seen his pale skin in the light, but she couldn't. All she could remember was that long, scraggly hair of his, him standing with a hunched and closed-off posture, and always with his hands in his pockets.

Always uncomfortable. Always *hiding*.

"But why?" Nora cried, surprised by sudden tears. "Why kill all of us?"

Julian didn't respond. He didn't even meet her eye.

"Because it's what vampires do," Proctor answered, and he did meet her eye. "Because we're his *enemy*. Because we're *werewolves.*"

If Nora's expression had been shocked before, it doubled in its intensity now. She stared at Proctor dumbfounded.

"W-what?" she stammered. "I don't—"

"It's all right, *hermana*," Proctor said, and he shook his head at her. "No need to deny it."

Nora just continued to stare. "How...how did you know?"

"Because they were too," the hunter said, motioning to the sheeted bodies on the floor. "Every last one of 'em, I think." His eyes went to the small, broken window. "We'll find out soon enough."

Nora followed his gaze and felt a chill run down her spine. Twilight was ebbing now, the world outside turned dim.

The full moon was close.

"At first, I thought I might've been the only one," Proctor continued. "But then the quarterback burned his hand on the fence—the *silver* fence—and I started thinking the odds were a bit funny. Add that actress setting herself ablaze on the thing, and I started thinking maybe those odds were a bit *too* funny."

Nora shuddered at the memory of Amelia's blackened corpse. And of Yusuf's bled one. She'd seen both of them burned by that silver barrier, and she'd simply chalked it up to the electricity. But then, electricity didn't burn...not like that anyway. No, Nora had seen burning like that—had felt it herself, even. Now that Proctor said it, it seemed so obvious. Why hadn't she seen it before?

"I started thinking about the letter we got," Proctor said, pulling an envelope from his pocket with a familiar red script on its front. "About how Ms. Wilmore said we all might share a 'similar interest.' Or how *he* did." He nodded to Julian again.

"So which was it, niño? Was *la mujer* a werewolf too? Or just another trick you used to get us here?"

"Y-you don't understand," Julian stammered. "I'm not...I didn't..." He trailed off, shaking his head at the ground.

"What?" Proctor demanded, still pointing the crossbow at Julian. "What don't I understand?"

Julian just continued to shake his head. His eyes were wide, and he looked about as scared as Nora had ever seen him, though he held fast to the knife in his hand. She noticed his eyes kept shifting around the room.

"You gotta give me something, kid," Proctor said, and Nora thought she heard a hint of regret in his voice. Though when Julian still refused to respond, the hunter just nodded.

"Fine then," he said, and fired the crossbow.

The shot was quieter than Nora expected, silenced maybe, though Julian screamed all the same. Nora turned to see what looked like a thin brown stake protruding from the boy's stomach. It was wooden, and it made Julian fall to his knees.

"Hurts, doesn't it?" Proctor said, approaching the boy. "Yeah, you vampires have never liked wood much. Burns you 'bout as bad as silver does us, though I'll let you in on something that might make you feel better."

He squatted down next to where Julian lay clutching his stomach, got in real close.

"That pain you're feeling right now? It's nothing compared to what the lady and I are going to be feeling in just a few minutes here." He threw a thumb at Nora then cocked it toward the window. "When that full moon goes up and the *change* happens, it's an agony like nothing you ever felt, hermano. Though you're bound to find out."

He hawked a wad of spit to the ground and got in even closer, inches away from Julian's face.

"When the change happens, when the lady and I turn and grow fangs of our own, you're bound to feel something *worse*."

Proctor stood back up, sent the knife Julian had dropped on the ground skidding into the corner, then turned to Nora.

"They might turn too, you know," he said, nodding again to the sheeted bodies.

"Right," Nora said, nodding back. It was a tricky thing when werewolves died around the rising of a full moon. Whether or not they would undergo a final change was always uncertain.

"Odds are we'll be able to clear that fence once we've turned, jump that silver pen and leave Wilmore Manor behind. Though I don't envy the one who finds it next." He looked slowly around the room they stood in. "Four werewolves and a vampire dead in the basement. Plus the professor upstairs and the actress out front." He shook his head. "I wonder what they'll make of it."

Proctor had the trace of a grin on his lips, though Nora didn't. She was too busy recounting the bodies in the room, recounting the details.

"Four?" she said, and the alarm in her voice must have been clear, for Proctor's grin vanished, and his eyes immediately went to the floor. There were four bodies all right, though something was off. Something they hadn't noticed before.

"Shouldn't...shouldn't there be five?" Nora said, and this made Proctor's eyes go wide.

Suddenly, Julian was moving.

"I'm sorry," he whimpered, trying and failing to rise to his feet. Nora realized he was crying. "I'm so *sorry*."

"What did you do?" Proctor demanded, seizing the boy by his collar. Julian let out a cry of pain as he was pulled upright.

"Please..." he said, voice barely a whisper. "Please don't."

Proctor's crossbow was at his throat, though Julian wasn't looking at the hunter, didn't even seem to be speaking to him, Nora realized.

She turned to the shadowy opposite side of the basement, and that's when she saw it.

There was something within those shadows, something staring back at her. It peered out of the darkness with small, upside-down eyes, and then it screeched.

With a leathery flutter, it emerged from the blackness, and Proctor turned too late.

What had been a small black bat turned, in an instant, into a full-sized woman. Black-haired, dark-skinned, and entirely naked, Nora realized with shock that it was a woman she knew. Her eyes were open now, and her throat no longer bore a bloody scar, though their mysterious, murdered host was as recognizable as ever.

Valentina Wilmore lunged forward, and sank long white fangs into the side of Proctor's neck.

The hunter never stood a chance. None of them had, Nora realized now. Amelia had been right when she'd said it before; they'd been doomed from the very start.

As Proctor's body went limp, eyes wide as the naked woman made horrible gnashing sounds at his neck, the crossbow fell from his grip and hit the floor with a clatter.

Nora did not stop to think. Adrenaline pumping, and the moon drawing near, she lunged for it, though she was not quick enough.

No sooner had she taken a step forward than did Valentina appear before her, inhumanly fast, bringing a searing pain along with her. A wave of agony shot through Nora's chest suddenly, and a delayed cry from Julian told her the cause. The wooden stake no longer protruded from the boy. Valentina had ripped it out and stabbed Nora instead.

She fell to her knees, mildly aware of a faint sizzling sound in her ears, though the pain drowned out much. It wasn't until Valentina stepped back, over the corpse of the hunter behind her, that Nora realized where the sound came from.

The bare woman's palm was bubbling, burning at the skin where she'd gripped the stake. It gave off the same, putrid aroma as had Amelia and Yusuf's silver burns, though Nora thought this smelled worse. For a moment, Valentina hissed at the injury, baring her fangs like a cat at her palm before letting it fall to her side. Her eyes then met Nora's, and a smile curled up her lips.

"A wooden stake through the heart," she said. Her voice was milky and heavily accented. "The only way to kill a vampire, they say." She smiled wider, and those long white fangs gleamed with red. "I find it works for everyone."

Her eyes flashed. "Even *werewolves*."

Nora's only reply was a hiccup of blood. It was becoming harder and harder to breathe, and parts of her had gone cold. She found herself looking toward the window, looking for the moonlight.

"Go on then," Valentina said, turning to Julian. She nodded to the crossbow still by Proctor's side. "Finish it." She looked to the window herself. "Before the moon rises and you make a mess of things."

Nora tried to move, tried to get up, but her muscles screamed in protest. The stake through her chest held her to the floor like an anchor, making it so that all she could do was wait.

She didn't have to long.

With obvious discomfort, Julian pushed himself to his feet, managing a feat Nora would have thought impossible in light of his injuries, though as the young man stepped closer, she began to notice a discernable difference between him and the vampire woman. Unlike Valentina's palm, the boy's midsection did not smoke or sizzle. It was as if the stake had not burned him like it had her, or even at all. Nora's shock and confusion, already abundant, doubled as Julian picked up the crossbow. Despite it being of an almost entirely wooden make, the boy did not so much as flinch.

"Y-you're not a vampire?" she managed.

What are you then? is the question she wanted to ask next, though a new wave of pain prevented her from doing anything more than groan.

Ultimately, Julian's eyes answered for him. They darted to the window with the same nervous anticipation hers did, the way every werewolf's did when the full moon was close. The revelation sent what little warmth Nora had left plummeting.

"You're...you're a *werewolf*?" she whispered, horrified. "But...but how?" She shook her head. "But *why*?"

She thought of them. Of Elijah and Nicholas, of Amelia and Yusuf, of Rowan and Damian, of Proctor. She thought of all of them. All of them who had come to this place in search of their kin. In search of brothers and sisters...only to be betrayed.

Why?

She was crying now, and Julian was too. He had been the whole time, she realized. He held the crossbow before her with trembling hands, though he did not use it.

Over his shoulder, Valentina emerged from the shadows like a dark specter.

"Do it," she whispered.

Julian took an unsteady step forward, shaking his head all the while. "I'm sorry," he sobbed. "I'm so sorry."

And then he did it.

Chapter Twelve

The End

The next morning found Julian in the study. His body ached like it always did the day after a full moon, though this time it was worse. This time, it was not just his muscles and bones which pained him.

Valentina Wilmore sat before him, fully clothed now, and working diligently on something at her desk. He'd entered a few moments ago, though the dark-haired woman had yet to address him. For a moment, he wondered if she had even noticed him. It was near pitch-black with the blinds closed, and with nothing but the yellow glow of a desk lamp to penetrate the shadows, Julian thought he might just be totally concealed, though he quickly thought better.

Dim as it was, the room was not so dark that certain details could not be made out.

Julian's own gaze kept drifting to a particular spot on the floor. Damian's body had been removed, though the stains where his and Elijah's blood had darkened the carpet remained as repulsive reminders of how each man had fallen.

The sight of those blotchy shapes made Julian sick, and so he looked away, turned his gaze to Valentina instead. The vampire must have sensed him looking, for she turned her head up soon after, eyes bright in the shadows.

"Julian," she said, in such a light, jovial tone that Julian felt a chill run up his spine. "How was your night?"

"Fine," he said, instinctively shoving his hands deep in his pockets. "Long."

"I appreciate your staying within the bounds of the property," she said with a nod. "Had you left, I fear you would have gone without your earnings."

She rose then, rounded the desk with slow, silent steps. A dark backpack hung from her arm, and Julian eyed it carefully.

"Is that it?" he asked, nodding to the pack.

Valentina nodded back.

"How much?"

"Eight million as we agreed," she said, brandishing it forth. Julian made to grab it, but Valentina pulled it right back.

"Though I wonder if you should get only *six*," she said, holding the bag just out of reach. There was a horrible smirk on her face.

"The job's done, isn't it?" Julian said, eyeing the woman carefully. He could feel his heart beating in his chest. "Eight million for eight dead."

"Yes, but only six of those eight died by your hand. I took the hunter, and the actress killed herself." The vampire's grin widened now, though Julian did not return it.

Finally, she thrust the bag forward.

"I am only kidding," she said, and Julian took a half step back as he caught the bag at his chest. It was heavier than he'd expected.

"You did marvelously," Valentina continued, and she was beaming at him now. "You have quite the talent for killing, you know. More so than any of my previous hands. Should you be interested in participating again—"

"No," Julian said suddenly, and more forcefully than he'd expected. He met Valentina's eyes, though the steel in them forced his gaze away. He shook his head.

"I'm sorry...but no. I can't." He met her eye again. "I *won't*."

For a long, disquieting moment, the vampire just stared at him. Then her smile returned.

"Very well," she said with a shrug, and turned back to her desk.

Julian was left to stare wide-eyed, heart still hammering in his chest. He forced a swallow.

"So, that's it?" he said. "You'll just let me go?"

"You'll find that the front gate is now open," she said, not even turning to look at him. Though when Julian still refused to move, she sighed.

Her eyes met his. "Yes?"

"Y-you're not going to kill me?" Julian asked, and he could not stop the stammer in his voice.

Valentina laughed. "Kill you? Why on earth would I do that?"

"You killed the other werewolves...why not me?"

"Because we had an agreement," Valentina said, and she nodded to the bag in his hands. "In addition to payment, your work this weekend rewards safety." She shot him a fangy smile. "I told you before that I wouldn't kill you, Julian. Didn't you believe me?"

Julian did not reply.

Valentina shrugged again. "I suppose your doubt is only natural. Though, as I believe the contents of that bag will assure you, I am a woman of my word."

Julian still didn't trust her, though the bag was heavy, and unzipping it revealed piles of green bills within. Eventually, he began to nod.

"Okay..." he said slowly. "Okay."

He looked back up, though Valentina had already returned her attention to her desk. It seemed the vampire had grown bored of him. He decided to leave before she changed her mind.

When stepping toward the door caused no change in the dark-haired woman's demeanor, Julian felt his nerves ease up a bit. Perhaps he *would* make it out of here alive.

Though his instincts were screaming at him to get as far away as possible as fast as possible, he stopped at the threshold all the same.

"Why?" was the single word he said, and this time, it was Valentina who looked up first.

"I'm sorry?"

"Why?" he repeated, turning to face her. His eyes had more than adjusted to the shadows by now, though the vampire still had a way of blending in. He shook his head. "Why not just kill them yourself? Or all of us, even?" His throat hitched, and the last words came out as a whisper. "Why use me?"

Valentina Wilmore did not offer him a smile this time, did not offer him anything but a cold stare and a tone ripe with grim determination.

"Because werewolves like you are the key, Julian. Werewolves who will betray their kind for the right reasons. For the right *price*. It's werewolves like you who will sow the seeds of mistrust across your entire species. And once enough grows, we vampires won't need concern ourselves with your eradication, with *killing* you." Valentina shook her head, and a ghost of that fangy smile returned. "You'll all be too busy killing yourselves."

Even if Julian had thought of something to say, he was not sure that he could have said it. The pain in his stomach, there all along, had reared up again, was all but constricting the air in his lungs with its intensity.

"Off you go, then," Valentina said, nodding to the door, and her eyes returned to her desk. "I've letters to write."

***

Julian had made it maybe two miles from Wilmore Manor when his shirt gave way.

Having been first punctured by Proctor's stake, then further torn when Julian had turned with the moon, the purple Willy Wolfgang's staff tee had been on its last legs for some time now. Sick of it chafing under the weight of his backpack, Julian finally decided to just rip the entire thing off.

He did so savagely, with a hot rage that had been slowly building all morning. All weekend. After tearing every last thread of it from his body, he threw the remains to the ground where they landed in a pathetic pile. Within those purple folds, the gray face of Willy Wolfgang was left to stare up at him distortedly.

Julian stared back for a long time, stared alone in the woods, shirtless with a bag of money on his back, just looking at that cartoon wolf leering through the creases and holes.

Eventually, Julian walked on, though he didn't take the shirt with him. He couldn't stand the sight of it.

About the Author

Kieran Wiesenberg is an indie author from western New York.
Find out more at kieranwiesenberg.com

Also By Kieran Wiesenberg

The Arcane Amnesiac

Fearnomena

Darsimeon Gone

www.ingramcontent.com/pod-product-compliance
Lightning Source LLC
LaVergne TN
LVHW090523110826
845146LV00003B/963

* 9 7 9 8 9 8 6 0 0 0 7 3 2 *